IT WAS GOI

Jackson Fowler hit the pavement running, with the strike team on his heels. The point man brought the doorman down with a flying tackle, and Fowler stormed through the entrance, with reinforcements close behind.

As they neared a door marked Private, there was a sudden burst of gunfire, muffled by the walls but clearly audible. A heartbeat later the door was flung open to reveal a slender Cuban with a Tec-9 semiauto pistol in his hand.

He pulled up short and aimed the awesome-looking weapon straight at Fowler, but he never got the chance to fire.

Fowler favored double-ought for knockdown power when he had to fall back on a scattergun, and a dozen holes at point-blank range was enough for any man.

The Cuban took it in the chest and vaulted backward just as one of his team unleashed a stream of automatic fire.

A couple of the strike team members blasted the gunman with their M-16s, and Fowler watched him come apart.

''Enough!'' he shouted, but the rest of them were gone before he reached the open door....

AGENTS

TRIGGER PULL

PAUL MALONE

A GOLD EAGLE BOOK FROM

WORLDWIDE®

TORONTO · NEW YORK · LONDON · PARIS
AMSTERDAM · STOCKHOLM · HAMBURG
ATHENS · MILAN · TOKYO · SYDNEY

First edition May 1991

ISBN 0-373-63801-9

Special thanks and acknowledgment to
Mike Newton for his contribution to this work.

TRIGGER PULL

TRIGGER PULL

PROLOGUE

The prowler took no chances going in. His turtleneck and jeans were black, as were his leather gloves, his watch cap and his brand-name running shoes. The blue-steel automatic on his hip was covered by a Lo-Ride canvas holster, the Bianchi special, and his face was blackened by a layer of army surplus camo paint. The jet-black Nikon hanging on a strap around his neck was waterproof and carried high-speed, infrared film.

He felt like Rambo Junior, but embarrassment was nothing in comparison to what would happen if the hardguys made him on the probe.

For starters, Coral Gables lay outside his jurisdiction. He had no authority to cross the line, and his superiors would not be satisfied to disavow him if the mission blew up in his face. In fact, they would be lining up three-deep to crucify his ass.

Official sanctions hardly mattered, though, since any foul-up meant exposure to the enemy, and that in turn meant instant death.

Or not so instant, if the boys were in a mood for fun and games.

The automatic was a last resort, but going in unarmed was suicide. At least this way he had a fighting chance if he was blown.

The target was a high-priced layout on Granada Boulevard, four acres abutting the canal, a short hike from the Riviera Golf Course. He approached in true commando style, complete with rubber boat to get him there and back again.

The preparation had been fairly simple, but it wasn't free. A double C note and a loose-lipped rent-a-cop provided all the information he required about security. No motion sensors on the grounds. No dogs. No voltage in the chain-link fence with coils or razor wire on top. As dealers went, his mark was living almost recklessly.

The guards were something else, and he would have to work around them in the dark, avoiding contact. They were paid to shoot on sight and never mind the questions, a defensive posture that had managed to insure their boss's privacy...so far.

He double-checked the fence for an electric charge, in case the informant was shucking him, then cut himself a gate and wriggled through. Inside he lingered long enough to close the flap with twist ties so that it would pass a cursory inspection in the dark. That done, he scanned for roving sentries, saw none in sight and made a scuttling beeline for the house.

He could not peg the style to save his soul. Some kind of Spanish classical with new additions in the space-age mode, with jagged angles, yards of tinted glass and cool pastels.

The carport held a classic Jaguar and a gray Mercedes, while a white stretch limo blocked the drive in front. Behind it, looking shabby as a poor relation at a formal banquet, sat a two-door Dodge the prowler recognized.

All systems go.

He kept his distance from the lighted swimming pool— no careless silhouettes to give himself away—and started counting heads inside the sunken living room, behind glass sliding doors. The dealer was holding court with his subordinates, a new face here and there among the old.

The silent intruder was too far for an effective shot. Creeping on hands and knees across the patio he came up beside a redbrick barbecue and palmed the Nikon's lens cap, zooming in to focus on the dealer's profile first. A wider angle would include the others, one face in particular. Then he'd have them in the bag.

The prowler could not read their lips, and while the snapshots might not stand in court, they were enough for a review board to demand some answers. Even if the secondary target wriggled out from under charges, he would still be facing microscopic scrutiny until the day he pulled the pin.

It was a start.

The Nikon's automatic drive produced a tiny whirring sound as he began to shoot, enough to help disguise the sound of footsteps on his flank.

But not the voice.

"Hands up, *cabrón*."

He dropped the camera on his chest and raised both hands, shifting his line of vision toward the Uzi submachine gun that was leveled at his face from twenty feet away. The odds were shitty, but he was prepared to try it anyway... until a second gunner turned up on his left.

They had him in a cross fire, and he could only wonder why he wasn't dead.

"The gun, *pendejo*. Nice and easy, slide it over here."

He did as he was told, the automatic scraping over tile and stopping short between the gunner's feet.

"The camera, now."

It didn't slide as well. The gunman had to stretch a bit, but he was satisfied.

"Facedown, and spread your arms like *Jesucristo*. Any tricks, you learn to walk without your knees."

Spread-eagle, on the deck, he lay immobile while the second shooter turned his pockets out and checked for backup weapons, finally satisfied that he was clean. He had been careful not to carry his ID, though at this point it made no difference at all.

"Get up. We go inside."

They prodded him across the wide veranda and around the corner to a servants' entrance, through the kitchen and along a pastel corridor to reach the sunken living room. A ring of faces gaped at him, caught between surprise and anger as they looked him over.

"Keegan!"

Glancing over at his guest, the dealer frowned. "You know this man?"

"He's one of mine."

The prowler dropped his hands. "I'd have to disagree with you on that, Lieutenant."

"Smart bastard!"

"Not so smart, I guess."

"You got that right, you shit."

The dealer silenced his accomplice with a glance. He took the prowler's automatic and the Nikon from his watchdog, weighing one in either hand, as though he was making up his mind which item he should buy.

"What brings you to my home?"

"Moonlighting for the network, asshole. You're on *Candid Camera*."

"Most amusing. I'll be interested to see how long your sense of humor lasts."

"I may surprise you."

"Let's find out."

He knew that it was now or never. Two quick steps to reach the gunner on his left, an elbow shot to the esophagus, and he put all his weight behind a twist to jerk the automatic rifle free. His finger on the trigger, he was pivoting to spray his adversaries when the Uzi stuttered. He sat down hard, the rifle spinning from his hands.

His shocked gaze strayed to the beige ceiling tiles. They reminded him of photographs from outer space, the pitted surface of the moon.

He drew a ragged breath and waited for the pain.

The gunner loomed above him, looking ten feet tall instead of five-foot-nothing in his pointy cowboy boots.

"He's still alive, *patrón.*"

Then the lieutenant stepped up beside him, with his right hand wrapped around a shiny automatic.

"Guess again."

Mean streets, Jack Fowler thought contemptuously, hunched down inside the confiscated van on Calle Ocho. The guy who coined the term was probably a trendy film producer from Beverly Hills whose idea of adventure was negotiating side streets off Rodeo Drive. For damn sure, the portrayals coming out of Hollywood in recent years had no more contact with reality than Roger Rabbit— and the nightly doses of crapola from the media were often just as bad.

As mean streets went, Miami's Calle Ocho ranked around a five or six on Fowler's private ten-point scale. The merchants were sedate enough, all Cuban and conservative and anti-Castro, but the action that concerned Jack Fowler seldom took place in bodegas or boutiques. It went down for the most part in cafés and nightclubs, in apartments set back from the boulevard . . . or on the street itself.

Miami's Eighth Street pierced the heart of Little Havana like a well-aimed arrow, skewering the dreams of several hundred thousand immigrants Dade County had collected over thirty years. They came initially as short-term refugees from Castro's revolution, scheming with the CIA and spinning fantasies of *Cuba libre* that were tough to kill. A later generation came from Mariel, released from Castro's prisons and asylums in a gesture toward "humanitarian relief." Their dreams were different—instant fame and fortune in the Land of Opportunity—and they pursued it with a ruthless vigor that ignored established laws and mores.

Enter Jackson Fowler and the DEA.

Cocaine had fueled Miami's crime wave since the latter 1970s, and there was still no end in sight, despite sporadic declarations and renewals of a federal war on drugs. Around southern Florida, street agents took the action one day at a time and did their best to weed out hopeless dreams of final, sweeping victory.

This afternoon, Jack Fowler would have settled for a decent score. He sat and watched the spinning reels of tape, one losing weight, the other getting fat, as a technician wearing headphones gave the play-by-play.

"They're in," he said at last, referring to Gutierrez and Ybarra, pausing as the undercover agents waded through a round of introductions in the back room of a Cuban nightclub, just across the street and midway down the block.

"Here's Santiago, now."

Guillermo Santiago was the target of the evening. He was linked with distribution of Colombian cocaine between Miami and Savannah, pulling down an estimated net of thirteen million tax-free dollars in the past twelve months. Tonight he would be talking weights and measures with the "Carioca brothers," veteran stingers from the Tampa office of the DEA, on loan to the Miami hutch as virgin faces on the scene.

Jack checked his watch and shifted slightly on the jump seat, wishing he could stretch his legs out in the crowded van. Besides the sound man, he was sharing quarters with a four-man strike team huddled over riot guns and automatic rifles as they waited for the word—a ring of poker faces, none of them revealing what he felt inside.

"That's it!" the sound man snapped. "It's going down!"

Already moving toward the double doors, Jack raised the compact walkie-talkie to his lips and barked, "Move in! Repeat, move in!" He hit the pavement running, with the strike team on his heels, the startled driver of a racy sports car standing on his brakes and cursing as they charged across the street. While traffic swerved, amid the exasperated blowing of horns and the screeching of rubber, Fowler focused on his target and the figures of converging shock troops closing in.

They had a six-man team in back to seal the logical escape hatch, snipers on a roof across the street in the event that Santiago's people had an ambush waiting in the wings. On paper it looked like overkill, but in this profession no one reached retirement age by taking chances on the street.

The doorman saw them coming. He turned to duck inside and trigger the alarm before Jack's pointman tackled him and brought him down. The guy was cuffed and out of it when Fowler reached the entrance, bursting through with reinforcements close behind.

The weekday crowd was spotty, ninety-eight percent Latino, with a couple of blacks thrown in to keep it cosmopolitan. Nobody raised a hand to stop them as they cut through strains of salsa from the jukebox, homing in on Santiago's private office in the back.

As they neared the door marked Private, they heard a sudden burst of gunfire, muffled by the walls but clearly audible. A heartbeat later, the door burst open to expel a slender Cuban with a Tec-9 semiauto pistol in his hand. He pulled up short and aimed the awesome-looking weapon at Fowler, but he never got the chance to fire a single shot from the 36-round magazine.

Ballistics experts had decided number-four shot was the optimum in combat shotgun rounds, but Fowler favored double-ought for knockdown power when he had to fall back on the scattergun. Each Magnum round contained a dozen pellets, each the approximate size and weight of a .32-caliber pistol bullet—and a dozen holes at point-blank range was generally enough for any man.

The Cuban *pistolero* took it in the chest and vaulted backward, dead before he hit the nearest wall where he left a crimson skid mark on the stucco. Fowler worked the shotgun's slide and crossed the threshold in a fighting crouch, aware of bodies on the floor and others moving toward an exit to his left.

One of the bodies lay facedown, arms raised as if to help contain a spreading pool of blood. Jack did not recognize the clothing, but he made out number two, all right. Gutierrez was curled up on his side and clutching at the place where one or more hot rounds had pierced his abdomen. The guy was still alive, his partner crouched beside him, squeezing off a round at the retreating gang.

One of the Santiago team unleashed a burst of automatic fire, the bullets crackling overhead and bringing down a rain of plaster dust. Ybarra shot him twice before a couple of the strike team members joined the party, blasting him with M-16s as Fowler watched him come apart.

"Enough!" he shouted, but the rest of them were gone before he reached the open door. Dark corridor stretched beyond, and then another doorway, standing open on a dimly lighted alleyway.

Another burst of firing told him that the back-door team was kicking in, surprised by Santiago's fighting exit but responding as they had been taught. Jack slowed his pace, emerging from the safety of the corridor into a cross fire. Santiago and a couple of his soldiers were pinned behind a Dumpster in the alley, cut off short of access to the El Dorado they had waiting several paces farther on. A couple of the strike team guys were down but moving, their companions heatedly returning fire with everything they had.

One of the Cubans broke from cover, blasting with an Uzi as he started for the Cadillac. Behind him, Santiago and his other stooge provided cover fire, prepared to follow if their pointman reached the car alive.

He almost made it, one hand on the door latch when he caught a round between the shoulder blades and staggered, slumping against the Caddy as he went down. If Santiago felt the loss of one more friend, it didn't show. Instead he grabbed his sole surviving comrade by the shirt and shoved him toward the El Dorado, squeezing off two hasty rounds from what appeared to be a Desert Eagle .44.

The runner stumbled, taken by surprise, and someone hit him with a burst of automatic fire before he got his balance back. The impact punched him through a sloppy pirouette and dropped him on the pavement in a twitching pile.

Surrounded, hopelessly outnumbered, Santiago saw the writing on the wall. He pitched his automatic from behind the Dumpster, calling out, first in Spanish then English, his intention to surrender. Fowler had the dealer covered as he rose, one hand above his head, the other hanging limp against his side.

"I'm hit," the dealer called to no one in particular. "Somebody take me to the hospital."

Uninjured members of the raiding party were on their feet, closing in on Santiago as he showed himself. Their guards relaxed just a fraction in the presence of an unarmed, wounded man.

And Fowler saw the stubby pistol drop from nowhere, hidden in the sleeve of Santiago's jacket on a spring or whatever, waiting for a do-or-die emergency.

Like now.

He saw the dealer's gun hand rising, spitting fire, and another member of the strike team going down. The shotgun bucked against his shoulder, and the muzzle-flash obscured Santiago's profile for an instant, but it was gone in time for Jack to see his target blur, spewing blood and pitching out of frame. The dealer went down like a sack of laundry, sprawling flaccid on the ground.

Around him, men were in motion, patting down the fallen hoods for weapons, taking inventory of the dead and wounded. Fowler felt a presence at his elbow and turned to confront Ybarra.

"How's Gutierrez?"

"He's been better, but I think he'll make it. Santiago?"

"Over there. He had a little accident."

Ybarra cracked a smile and said, "It couldn't happen to a nicer guy."

2

The call from Rudy Stano had to be bad news. It was a flagrant breach of field security, with an assignment underway, and Jackson Fowler knew that his control would not have risked it under normal circumstances. Worse, a summons to the Federal Building meant that Stano thought his present cover was expendable, a hint of something ugly in the wind.

He had been working overtime with Paul Enriquez for the past ten days to get a handle on a street gang dealing crack in the vicinity of Dorsey Park. The dealers ranged in age from seventeen to twenty-five, and they had murdered five of their competitors in seven months. The last known victim, age nineteen, had been decapitated, with his severed head displayed atop a corner mailbox near his parents' home.

They had been getting closer, starting from a routine purchase on the street and working up to greater weight. The next step was a parley for a major deal, with Fowler and Enriquez hanging tough on their demand for meetings with the men in charge. From that point, once the cash changed hands, they would be sitting on enough hard evidence to put the whole damned crew away.

Unless somebody scuttled it.

Like now.

Miami's Federal Building stood on Flagler Street, a mile due east of Biscayne Bay. It occupied a corner lot and filled up half a block, from north to south, a high rise that housed agents of the FBI and IRS, probation officers and the United States attorney's office, federal marshals, Health and Human Services, along with various recruiters for the Army, Air Force, Navy and Marines. The southeast corner of the seventh floor was occupied by Florida division offices of the Drug Enforcement Administration, covering activities of ten resident offices throughout the state.

A parking space was waiting for him in the underground garage, and Fowler locked his vintage Camaro, taking time to activate the tamper-proof alarm. He wasn't counting on any trouble at that spot . . . but then again, Colombia's ex-minister of justice had not counted on assassins trailing him from Medellín to Budapest, eight thousand miles away.

It was a trifle late to take precautions after you were planted in the ground.

The average citizen, confronted with an audit by the IRS or hassling a problem with his Social Security checks, would never know that he was under careful scrutiny, by men and cameras, from the moment he set foot across the threshold of the Federal Building's lobby. If his business took him higher than the fourth-floor office of Internal Revenue, he would be greeted on arrival by a U.S. marshal who inquired about the nature of his business, scanned his bod and any baggage for potential weapons with a beeper wand and sent him on his way.

Jack Fowler had his DEA ID in hand before he reached the seventh floor, the marshal double-checking with a list he carried on a metal clipboard certified to stop a .45 round fired at point-blank range. He didn't need directions to the office, but he got them anyway, and thanked the marshal with a smile.

It felt like working for the CIA sometimes, but Fowler knew employees of the Company had less to fear from hostile spooks in East Berlin than drug enforcement agents did in southern Florida—or anywhere around the

world, when it came down to that. The average DEA recruit would face a lethal situation, weapons drawn,
within a week of graduation from the Quantico academy. Not all of them would walk away.

The secretary handling Stano's calls was blond, late
twenties, new since Fowler's last appearance on the seventh floor. Though she did not know his face, she relaxed at sight of the ID protruding from his pocket, and
her left hand reappeared from underneath the desk to
join its slender mate.

Had she spooked and hit the panic button, Fowler
knew that every agent on the floor—together with the
marshals on the elevator—would have instantly responded with their weapons drawn. Preparedness for
armed attack had been a fact of life at DEA the past ten
years or so, since trigger-happy operators started heating
up the drug scene from a state of siege to all-out war.

"Yes, sir?"

"Jack Fowler, for the chief."

"One moment, please."

She phoned it in and cradled the receiver seconds later,
reaching for another button that would open Stano's
private door. When Rudy was away, the door would be
secured with an electric lock whose combination was unknown even to his secretary.

It was paranoia elevated to an art form and accepted
as a daily fact of life, an adjunct to survival when the
stakes were always life and death.

"Come in, Jack. Have a seat."

The secretary may have changed, but Rudy Stano
looked the same. Five-ten and stocky, eyes like flint, his
sandy hair revealing hints of gray. His suit and office
smelled of the cigars he favored, purchased from a shop
on Calle Ocho, in a neighborhood where several different dealers had a standing price on Rudy's head.

"So fuck 'em," he would say if anyone brought up the question of propriety. "I'm armed, I've got security devices up the ying-yang at my home and office. Now you're telling me I shouldn't go outside? Get real."

A full-time narc for twenty years, he had transferred to DEA in 1973 when the old Bureau of Narcotics and Dangerous Drugs was dissolved. As a participant in the original French Connection bust, Stano enjoyed a certain celebrity status in the service, but he never rested on his laurels. In fact, he seldom rested *period,* continually driving agents under his command toward bigger and bigger confiscations, more and better field arrests.

"Right now you're wondering if I've gone crazy. Am I right?"

"It crossed my mind."

"You're working an important job, it's almost there . . . and here we are."

"I'm listening."

There was no apprehension yet in Fowler's mind. He believed in not borrowing grief, especially when there was usually enough to go around.

"Glen Keegan."

"What about him, Rudy?"

Stano's frown was carving furrows in the tan slabs of his cheeks. "When was the last time that you saw him, Jack?"

"Six months or so. We had a few slow minutes on a Sunday, I recall."

"He seem all right to you?"

"I'd say. We had a couple steaks and put some beer away. Talked shop."

"Specifics?"

"Nothing off the top. If this is leading somewhere—"

"Keegan's dead."

"Say *what?*"

"They found him in the river by the Customs House at nine o'clock this morning. Guy was fishing, and he thought he hooked the big one. Freaked him out when he reeled Keegan in."

"What happened, Rudy?"

"M.E.'s still composing his report, but we've confirmed a death by gunshot—multiples, that is. No solid suspects, nothing on the scene. Fact is, they can't say where he hit the water."

"Do they have an estimate on time at least?"

"Last night for sure. They're doing what they can with the specifics."

"Jesus."

"You guys were tight, I understand."

"Four with Metro, yeah. I'd say that we were pretty close."

"How come he didn't make the move when you did?" Stano asked.

"With Glen, you took a job, you ought to finish it, no matter what. He saw the same crap going down that I did, but he had the notion he could fix things starting from the inside."

"A whistle-blower?"

"Not in my experience."

"Times change."

"Is that supposed to tell me something?"

"Jack, you know we try to keep in touch with Metro-Dade."

"The ones that you can trust."

"Correct. The rumble is that Keegan had some kind of line on rotten apples in the Narco squad. If what I'm hearing is correct, these guys would make the river cops look like a bunch of Boy Scouts."

Everybody in Miami knew about the river cops, a gang of seven officers arrested during 1985 on federal counts of racketeering and conspiracy. Their scam was relatively simple, stealing dope obtained as evidence for future trials and then reselling it, or ripping off street dealers at the source. The latter action led to several homicides, and other hits were in the works when agents of the DEA and FBI closed in to drop the net. By that time, all the river cops were millionaires; they could afford the best in legal talent—plus the bribes that finally resulted in a mistrial culminating in 1986.

"You know that much," said Fowler evenly, "there must be more."

"No names, unfortunately. Keegan kept the hot stuff to himself and watched his back . . . at least he did until last night. The way I hear it, secondhand, he had it in his mind to finger a command-grade officer who's cozy with Rodriguez."

"Damn!"

"I'd say that sums it up, all right."

Jorge Luis Rodriguez was the cream of cocaine dealers in Miami, powerfully connected with the Cali-Medellín cartels and never short of product on the street. His record listed ten or fifteen busts and one conviction, on a charge of driving his Mercedes while intoxicated and without an operator's license. He had paid a small fine and walked away.

It was a point of common knowledge that Rodriguez had his own keen eyes at Metro-Dade, a crucial edge that tipped him off to sweeps and raids with time enough to wash his hands before the troops arrived. Persistent rumors had it that Rodriguez could adjust an officer's assignment if the uniform in question gave him too much heat, but nothing had been proved. If anyone could groom a squad of renegades inside the force and make them dance on cue, Jorge Luis Rodriguez was the man.

"I want this, Rudy."

"Thought you might. Of course, there's still this other thing at Dorsey Park."

"Enriquez has been covering the meets," said Fowler. "These boys don't like gringos, anyway. A decent cover—say I got picked up on something, for example—and I don't believe they'd mind a nice Hispanic face, instead. Might even help the deal along."

"It has to be Paul's choice. I won't just leave him hanging so that you can play avenger, Jack."

"Okay."

"You'll have him call me?"

"Later on this afternoon."

"You won't do anything peculiar till we've had that talk?"

"Peculiar's not my style."

"I know your style. I turn you loose on this and pretty soon Rodriguez has an accident. We want this piece of shit in court."

"For killing Glen?"

"Whatever sticks, we'll take it, Jack."

"Like when he cuts himself a deal?"

"He'd have to give us someone bigger than himself. That thins the herd."

"I'd really hate to see him walk."

"Forget about it. Guys like this would rather die than talk."

"Suits me."

"It won't be open season, Jack."

"It never was."

"Just so you know. You're going home from here?"

"I ought to check on Molly first."

"That's the widow?"

"Right."

"Rough duty, passing on the word. I've done it two, three times, and that's enough."

"She may need something. I don't know."

"You won't forget Enriquez?"

"Not a chance."

"So hit the bricks already. I'll be back in touch."

"Nobody else," said Fowler, pausing at the door. "He's mine."

"We'll see. Goodbye, Jack."

There were no checks on the ride back down, since security clearly assumed that a ringer would have pulled whatever he had in mind before he left the building. Back in the garage, deactivating the alarm and slipping into his Camaro, Fowler tried to picture Molly Keegan as she had been when he'd seen her last.

He dreaded seeing her like this, but it was something he had to do. A debt to Glen and Molly, plus a challenge to himself, all rolled up into one. And he would need some time to think, to sort things out, before the hunt began in earnest.

Back at the academy, the DEA instructors always stressed that it was not a game, but lately Fowler thought they might be wrong. The more he looked around himself, the more he picked out losers everywhere and a few big winners raking in the chips like there was no tomorrow.

And for some, there wouldn't be.

Like Keegan.

You anted in and took your chances, raising to the limit when you saw an opportunity and folding with reluctance if the bloodshed came too close to home. Whenever possible, you made your mind a blank and didn't think about the odds.

But he was thinking now.

Rodriguez and his dirty cops had called the tune for a no-limit game, and Fowler would be happy to oblige.

The game was dead-man-out.

And all the cards were wild.

3

The funeral services were held at Woodlawn Park, adjacent to the Tamiami Trail, on the dividing line between Southwest Miami and Coral Gables. Fowler picked up Molly Keegan and her eight-year-old, a dark-haired boy named Tommy who possessed his father's eyes, and drove them to the cemetery, where a crowd of suits and uniforms had gathered to present their last respects.

He recognized a number of the faces from his days at Metro-Dade, when he and Glen were partners, but a lot of them were strangers. Fowler's eyes covertly searched each in turn for signs of guilty knowledge, hidden satisfaction or relief behind the mourning mask. It didn't follow automatically that Keegan's killers would be present at the funeral, but he couldn't rule it out.

Reactions to his presence at the widow's side were mixed. Some old-time friends glad-handed him within the limits of good taste. A few seemed openly resentful or suspicious of an ex-cop who had joined "the enemy" by switching his allegiance to the Feds, as if their mutual objectives had been altered somehow by the change of wording on a badge.

And there was visible resentment, too—or was it outright jealousy?—when Molly Keegan took his arm and leaned on him for support as Glen was lowered into the ground.

Actually, some of it was understandable, he thought. At thirty-six, she could have passed for ten years younger, even in her widow's weeds and without a trace of makeup on her face. The body, sheathed in black, was slim and softly rounded, subtly provocative in spite of the occasion. Knowing Molly Keegan was to want her, and a number of the mourners seemed to view Jack Fowler more as competition than a family friend and comforter in time of need.

In point of fact, he grudgingly admitted to himself that he was not unmoved by Molly's aura of unconscious sensuality. A hundred years ago, when he was still at the police academy, they had gone out on several dates before Jack introduced her to his future partner and the die was cast. As best man at their wedding, Fowler meant it when he wished them best of luck . . . but not without a touch of envy for the groom.

The Keegans had been separated and considering divorce when Glen was killed, a fact that certain cocksmen at the station house interpreted to mean that Molly was available to one and all. As she rebuffed each stud in turn, she earned a reputation as an ice queen, but Fowler thought he had an inkling of the truth.

It was the job.

She blamed police work for the damage to her marriage, and he could not say that she was wrong. Fear was a constant attendant on a job where each new day could be the last. There were long nights alone, with Glen unable or unwilling to discuss his whereabouts, and on the occasions when he did discuss the job, she was horrified.

But the fear was the worst, a solitary constant for the wife or husband of a law enforcement officer, when every traffic stop or family argument was a potential killing situation. In Narcotics, where the daily stakes ran into millions and the average dealer packed at least one submachine gun in his sporty BMW, the risks were multiplied a hundred times. In Homicide or Vice, a cop could put his twenty in and never draw his piece outside the

target range, but narcs were living in a different world—
a free-fire zone where muscle talked and bullshit walked.

Toss in the anger and frustration honest cops experi-
enced when dealing with a system that was visibly corrupt and skewed toward rich defendants with a battery of
high-priced legal talent, Fowler thought, and you had a
recipe for mood swings that was guaranteed to leave a
conscientious lawman brooding over modern justice,
even when he shed his uniform and headed home to
open, loving arms.

Cops dealt with disillusionment in different ways.
Some walked away and found themselves a new career in
real estate, used cars, insurance—anything to wash their
hands of law enforcement and begin afresh. Some went
along to get along, accepting cash to look the other way,
occasionally graduating into active roles as triggermen
and muscle for the slime they were supposed to put away.
Increasingly the honest cops went looking for another
way to buck the tide, with federal agencies that still
maintained a better record of integrity.

And some stood fast, like Keegan, working from
within to sweep their own house clean. It cost them in the
long run—even honest cops close ranks against the
whistle-blowers who embarrass the department—and a
few, like Keegan, paid the tab in blood.

Well, there were tabs and tabs, thought Fowler.
Sometimes paybacks were a bitch.

He tuned the preacher out and let his mind drift back
to days when he and Keegan worked Narcotics as a team,
before they went their separate ways. The friendship had
endured in altered form, but it had never really been the
same. Glen never thought of Fowler as a traitor to the
force, the way some did, but it was obvious he thought
Jack should have stayed around to slug it out.

One image he could not escape involved the night Glen saved his life and stopped a bullet for his pains. It was their second year in harness as a team, and they were trolling for a cocaine cowboy by the name of Guy Camacho, alternately picking off his runners and applying pressure to his customers, until they had enough for an indictment that would put the slug away. The night they went to pick him up, Camacho came out shooting. Fowler was just a little sluggish off the mark and smelling funeral wreaths when Keegan threw himself across the line of fire. It cost Glen three weeks off and several inches of his small intestine, but Camacho bought the farm.

The first time Keegan saved his life.

The first time Fowler killed a man.

It had not been the last.

Glen never held it over him, the way others might have, and he never called the marker in. As time went on, they helped each other out of bloody scrapes a dozen times, with neither keeping score, but Fowler never lost his private sense of obligation. And he never had a chance to pay Glen back in kind.

It was too late now.

But he could still do everything within his power to even up the score.

That didn't include vigilante moves, although the notion had a certain visceral appeal. Jack Fowler knew about the cops who stepped across the line and set themselves up as avengers of society, dispensing their idea of justice on the street. He understood their motives, the frustration, but he wasn't buying in.

Jorge Rodriguez and his bluesuit cronies had a debt to pay, but they would pay it by the book. Accumulated evidence, indictment and exposure via public trial, disgrace and ruin. Jail. With any luck at all, a holding cell at Raiford while they waited out appointments with the chair.

Of course, if they decided to resist arrest along the way...well, that would be a different story.

Blood for blood.

All by the book.

They did not wait around to see the grave filled in. The boy did not look weepy, but he appeared tired and strained. It took some time to disengage, with several dozen bluesuits and their wives delivering condolences along the way. Some offered hands to Fowler, others tried to stare him down, but most of them ignored him, a response that he found agreeable. It was a relatively short drive back to Molly's house on Poinciana—it had been the family home before their separation—but the silence made it drag.

The good news was that they found no mourners waiting for them at the house. Her closest living relative, an uncle, made his home in Colorado and could not afford the trip to see a stranger planted in the ground. Glen's aging father was a resident at a North Miami nursing home and barely knew what year it was; his doctors had agreed with Molly's judgment that announcing Keegan's death would be a waste of time.

Jack would have been content to leave them at the door, but Molly asked him in, and he could not refuse. The modest house felt empty, as though something was missing, even though he knew that Glen had been living in a small apartment on the northwest side for several months. His passing left a kind of vacuum all the same.

As soon as they made it past the front door, Tommy turned to his mother. "I'm going to my room, okay, Mom?"

"Hang your suit up for me?"

"Sure. I'll see you, Mr. Fowler."

"See you, Tommy."

He had never made the grade as Uncle Jack, and Fowler wondered if a trace of Keegan's disappointment in him had been transferred to the boy. If so, it would have been a subtle process, nothing conscious on Glen's part. Adults forgot the way that kids could pick up signals from a glance, a frown, a tone of voice.

Too bad we lose the talent as we grow, thought Fowler. Too damned bad we have to grow at all.

"Some coffee, Jack?"

"I'd better run."

"Nobody's chasing you," she said. "I'm having some. You're welcome."

"Well—"

"Sit down, okay?"

He sat and watched her move about the kitchen, a woman feminine but strong, all steel and velvet. Fowler thought he understood why Glen had never, to his knowledge, taken any of the offers of free sex from prostitutes or informants that were thrown at every cop from time to time. He didn't need to look for any action on the side...or maybe he was just afraid of losing what he had.

And wound up losing, anyway.

Embarrassed by stirrings of desire, Fowler shifted in his seat and glanced around the kitchen. Everything was in place and spotless, just the way he remembered. Glen had told him once that Molly could prepare a four-course meal by magic, whisking dirty pots and pans away before you had a chance to see them. Fowler wondered to himself how much of that was culinary skill and how much nervous energy, but he was not about to ask.

The coffee was delicious, and he told her so. He felt out of place, reduced to small talk with an old friend's widow in the middle of a Thursday afternoon.

"You loved him, didn't you?"

The question startled Fowler, coming out of nowhere.

"We were partners. Friends."

She shook her head. "It's more than that. He nearly quit, you know, a few weeks after you went federal."

"No. I mean, he never mentioned it."

"That's Glen. *Was* Glen." She dabbed an eye and kept the tremor from her voice. "It hurt him when you left, but he was never really angry. I believe he understood."

"I hope so."

"I was praying that he'd give it up, by then. It's stupid, but I used to blame the job for my miscarriage. I suppose he knew. He must have known."

The night that Molly lost their first child, in her fourteenth week of pregnancy, the Keegan-Fowler team was staking out a buy at the marina, watching cash and dope change hands. Glen came off shift, elated by the bust and seizure, to discover he had lost his unborn son.

"You may be right," he said. "About the job, I mean."

She shook her head again, her blond hair flashing highlights you could die for.

"No, I needed an excuse. Self-pity did the trick. I made myself believe that turning in his badge would roll back the clock and let us start from scratch."

"What changed his mind?"

"You want a laugh? I did." She sipped her coffee, smiling with a trace of bitterness. "The night I told him I was pregnant for the second time, I saw it in his eyes. He waited for a while before he told me he could never face our child unless he did his job. *I* killed him, Jack."

"That's bullshit, Molly. Glen was paid to put it on the line. You're not responsible for dirty cops and dealers any more than he was."

"I'm the one who made him stay. He felt he had to prove himself to me, to Tommy."

"Wrong again. One thing you have to know about Glen Keegan. No one ever made him do a thing he didn't want to do. He loved you very much, but there were other things at work inside his head. A sense of honor and responsibility. You want to blame somebody, don't go looking in a mirror. Point a finger at the bastards who deserve it."

"No one cares," she told him, sounding hollow. "All the brass this afternoon...his so-called friends in the department. Would you like to know how many of them have tried to talk me into bed since Glen moved out?"

Jack shook his head, remembering the faces and hating them.

"You never called me, Jack."

Instead of saying anything, he merely frowned.

"Sometimes—not often, mind you, but a *few* times— I imagined it was you on top of me when Glen and I were screwing."

"Jesus, Molly."

"Not when we were making love, you understand. There *is* a difference, Jack. But after Tommy, toward the end, we didn't make love anymore."

"I'm out of here."

"You're shocked. I'm sorry, Jack. That's really rather sweet."

"You're hurting, Molly. Give it time."

"Another secret for the road. You weren't half-bad."

Grief talking, Fowler told himself. He pushed his coffee cup away.

"I guess we'll never know."

"We might. You should have called me, Jack."

"I was his friend."

"And now?"

"I've got some bills to pay."

"Revenge?"

"Just picking up the pieces."

"Honor and responsibility. Look what they did for Glen."

"It cuts both ways."

"The difference is, your opposition doesn't give a damn. You take one out, a dozen others stand in line to fill his place. It's hopeless, Jack."

"If I believed that, I'd be selling ladies' lingerie."

"You'd make a killing. I could recommend you to my friends."

"I'll call you, Molly."

"When?"

"Tomorrow."

"What about tonight?"

"Take care of Tommy. He could use a shoulder."

"He could use his father, but it's too damned late for that."

The tears spilled over then, and Fowler moved around the table to take Molly in his arms. Her fists were clenched against his chest, her body rigid, but he felt her trembling inside. It took him by surprise when Molly raised her head and kissed him, a slow, searching kind of kiss that wanted a response.

Fowler knew he should have bolted, making tracks as fast as rubber legs could carry him, but it was she who broke the kiss, her cheeks on fire as she stepped back and turned away.

"I'm sorry, Jack. Forgive me, please."

"There's nothing to forgive."

"Tomorrow? Will you call me?"

"Yes."

He closed the screen door softly, worried she might shatter if he let it slam. Outside, the street and houses facing him looked sun-bleached, lifeless as a movie set when all the extras have gone home.

Walking to his car, he thought about Rodriguez and felt a momentary anger so intense it left a ringing in his ears. And he heard Molly's voice again.

Revenge?

Just picking up the pieces.

One of them was named Jorge Luis Rodriguez, but the others had no substance for him yet. He needed information first before he stumbled into something that could blow up in his face.

The skinny, right.

And Fowler knew that he would find it on the street.

4

To Jackson Fowler, working on narcotics in Miami felt like working in any other town in Florida or the United States. The dealers in Atlanta or Los Angeles would kill you just as quickly and without remorse. The street gangs, defending their illicit trade were as ruthless in Chicago and New York, Detroit or San Francisco. And, trendy TV shows aside, policing southern Florida remained primarily a matter of routine—surveillance, paperwork and dealing with informants or the crucial leads required to close a sticky case.

Snitches, good or bad, have been the backbone of American police work from the Salem witch trials to the present day. They are the eyes and ears authorities depend upon for information otherwise beyond their grasp, the final link in proving who did what to whom behind closed doors. The service they provide may be as simple as delivering an address where a wanted fugitive has gone to ground; in other cases, they may operate for years inside an outlaw syndicate, providing reams of information that will ultimately bring the structure down.

If there was any difference in Miami, it would be discovered in the quantity of snitches on the street. They ranged from petty thieves, junkies, prostitutes and pimps to top-rank dealers offering selective bits of information on their competition in return for leniency. The volume of narcotics traffic through Miami elevated snitching to the level of an art form or a cottage industry. Whole families survived—and sometimes died—by selling information on the fringes of the drug trade, dealing with police and sheriff's deputies, the DEA and Customs, FBI and IRS. They played no favorites, selling information to the dealers in their turn if there were profits to be made.

In four years with Narcotics, working Metro-Dade, Jack Fowler and his partner had recruited scores of snitches in Miami and environs. When Fowler made the move to DEA, they had continued sharing sources on a part-time basis, each developing his own leads on the side and trading off when it was practical. Some spies were more reliable than others, and a few had learned the hard way that you couldn't play both ends against the middle very long. From time to time, a street cop had to reevaluate his sources, making some changes here and there, discouraging operators who were prone to stretch the facts or sell themselves both ways.

Sometimes you wound up standing in a cemetery after everyone had gone—assuming anybody turned out for the service to begin with—staring at a brand-new grave and wondering exactly what went wrong.

Sometimes you knew and couldn't do a goddamned thing to put it right.

The best of snitches never worked for cash alone. They relished the intrigue and the adventure of a secret life, manipulating odds and living on the edge. You didn't have to ask if they were conscious of the dangers they were facing; you could see it in their eyes.

One such was Ricky Kastor, sometimes known as Rick the Stick for his preoccupation with the game of pool. A hustler in the truest sense, he had been running scams and con games since the age of twelve, a touch of smuggling on the side, and he had served three-quarters of a two-year jolt in county on a pimping charge years back. He still insisted that a kinky vice cop set him up, and Fowler was inclined to buy it, having known the officer in question and his penchant for suborning perjured testimony.

Still, poetic justice rolled around from time to time. The vice detective was himself convicted on a child-molesting beef a few months after Kastor made parole. It was reported that he did hard time, an ex-cop baby raper ranking well below informers on the inmate social scale. The afternoon he died at Raiford, doused with kerosene and set on fire by cons unknown, he had a meeting scheduled with the warden to request protective isolation for the balance of his term.

These days the Stick was mostly operating from a billiard hall he owned on Ludlam Road in South Miami, but his information net spread far and wide. He had his finger on the pulse of every major happening from Broward County to the Keys, and he would share that information when it suited him—first come, first served.

Jack Fowler knew enough to call ahead and fix a meet away from Kastor's place of business. Next to pool, the Stick liked racing best, and he suggested Hialeah Speedway since the bangtails would not run again for several weeks.

It was a stock car race that night, young men in loud machines, and a demolition derby afterward. The Stick was working on his second hot dog, chasing it with Coors, when Fowler took a seat beside him in the bleachers, way on top. Thinning hair and thirty extra pounds made the informer look a trifle soft.

"I heard about your partner."

"Former partner."

"Sure, that's what I meant to say. Damn shame. He was a decent guy."

"Too decent, maybe?"

"Such is life."

"The way I hear it, he was working on a link between Rodriguez and some guys at Metro-Dade."

"He wouldn't have to look too far."

It was the sorry truth. Statistics were a hopeless case, but few observers would deny that southern Florida was mired in official corruption unrivaled since Al Capone bought out Chicago in the Prohibition era. Soaring crime rates and minority action suits had prompted mass police recruitment in the early 1980s, doubling Miami's uniformed manpower in a two-year period. The downside was a visible relaxation of screening procedures and background checks, admitting dozens—some said hundreds—of suspected felons to the ranks of law enforcement, where they promptly set about collecting bribes, diverting confiscated drugs and weapons, strengthening their preexisting ties with major drug cartels. The handful of indicted river cops were not alone by any means.

"I'm looking for specific names," said Fowler, leaning close to Kastor so he didn't have to shout above the roar of engines.

"That's tricky. Way things are, you've got so many candidates to choose from, I'd need more to pin it down."

"We're not just talking temporary blindness with a shipment, or amnesia on the witness stand," said Fowler. "If I'm right, these guys are ripping off the small fry, maybe wasting some to make their point. Word is, they may have stepped on Keegan when he got too close."

"I wouldn't be surprised." The Stick was frowning at his hot dog, picking off a speck of something from the bun. "The kind of guys you're talking about don't take kindly to a knight in shining armor, if you get my drift."

"I don't mind taking chances."

"That makes one of us."

He recognized the dodge. The Stick was playing hard-to-get, not squeezing him exactly, but reminding Fowler of the risks involved.

"I didn't come to squeeze you, Ricky."

Kastor took another bite of hot dog, talking with his mouth full. "I remember one time Keegan helped me out when I was getting set up for a burn. Those Cubans—you remember the Chamasco brothers?"

"I remember."

"Fucking Louie was the big one, shoulders on him like a lineman for the Dolphins. Pumping all that iron upstate, I guess."

"They put it on."

"He's telling me they're gonna cut my head off— maybe put my sister on the street, some shit like that— unless I give them half my action on a little club I used to have those days."

"The Cockatoo, I think it was."

"You're right. I haven't thought about that place in years."

"It's just as well."

"It wasn't *that* bad."

"Well..."

"So Keegan comes around the night these assholes were supposed to make their first collection... have you heard this?"

"I believe I did."

The Stick went on nevertheless, seemingly talking to himself.

"There's Louie and his brother—I forget the little fucker's name—and they come in at closing time. They don't say shit to Keegan tending bar. Walk over, and they're in my face with all this crap about the money I'm supposed to owe, the vig and all."

"What happened?" Fowler asked, even though he knew.

The Stick was grinning. "Fucking *Keegan* happened, man. He came across the bar like he was trying out for the gymnastics team, but he was carrying a sawed-off baseball bat. That Louie hit the floor like forty pounds of goat shit in a gunnysack. Turned out his little brother was the tough one, but it didn't make no difference. Keegan whipped his ass and dumped them both out in the street. I thought for sure they'd wake up pissed, come back and burn me out, but Keegan says forget about it. Few days later, word came down the two of them were moving to Atlanta for their health.''

"About those names..."

"You have to understand, we're dealing with Rodriguez.''

"Right.''

"If it was someone else, it might be I could ask around and get a list, you know? Half dozen guys, or something you could handle. This Rodriguez now, he spreads the cream around. Some guys I talk to say he's greasing half the cops in town.''

"I don't believe that," Fowler said.

"I wouldn't know. My point is, reaching in the grab bag for some names—the heavies, even—isn't such a simple job.''

"But not impossible.''

Kastor shrugged, his meaty shoulders lifting underneath the flowered shirt.

"If it was me, I'd try to find myself a dealer with a grudge against Rodriguez. Somebody the cops you're looking for might try and squeeze. Turn on the charm, could be he'll whisper something in your ear.''

"That's all you've got?''

"I'll ask around some more. You understand, I have to be discreet.''

"Of course.''

He palmed a fifty, but the Stick ignored it, finishing his hot dog, washing down the last of it with beer.

"That Keegan, he was something else.''

"Okay. I'll see you, Stick."

"I wouldn't be surprised."

As he was coming down the stairs, one of the drivers lost control and kissed the wall, his right front wheel torn off and bouncing toward the infield with the stock car following, a plume of fire behind it like a comet's tail. The audience began to hoot and cheer, reminding Fowler of a bullfight he had witnessed once upon a time in Mexico.

He waited by the fence and watched until the burning stock car came to rest, the driver hopping out while fire extinguishers laid down a frosty cloud around the vehicle. A backward glance showed Fowler that where the Stick had been there was only a vacant seat with crumpled hot dog wrappers on the ground.

No sweat.

The guy was smart enough to cover for himself, and if he said that he would ask around, it was as good as done. A schemer all the way, he also had a reputation as a man who kept his word.

And it was personal.

His tale of Keegan whipping the Chamasco brothers had been Kastor's way of telling Fowler he had dues to pay. If there was information on the street, if Rick the Stick could run it down, the word would make its way to Fowler's ears.

But in the meantime, the Fed had work to do.

He had to find a dealer with a grudge against Rodriguez that was strong enough to make him break the code of silence, point the finger at a crooked cop or two. It would not have to stand in court, but Fowler needed names before he could begin his sweep.

He left the speedway, rolling south on West Sixteenth, and picked up Highway 27 southbound toward Miami. Fowler traveled half a mile before he made the tail, not

totally convinced until he caught the off ramp onto Hialeah Drive and swung around to Poinciana Boulevard
with the same car following his every move.

Okay.

If he was being tailed, it could mean one of several
things. Somebody shadowing the Stick on other business could be curious about their meeting at the speedway. Probably it was the police. The maze of Metro-Dade
had close to thirty local law enforcement agencies all told,
and any one of them might have a hard-on for the Stick.
But Fowler couldn't afford to have his plan exposed this
early in the game, when dirty cops made up a major seg-
ment of the suspect list.

Another possibility was that the Stick had a rumble
coming down with one of his competitors—something
Fowler didn't know about. It did not have to mean a drug
connection necessarily; more likely gambling, or a bit of
import-export on the side. The past few years, he knew
that Kastor had been moving gold from time to time,
some diamonds when he managed to connect, plus other
types of contraband. His major stock-in-trade was still
bolita—the Hispanic version of the numbers racket—
with assorted scams in real estate, insurance and securi-
ties. Whatever, getting burned with Kastor in an unre-
lated deal was not a part of Fowler's plan.

There was one final option, and he liked it least of all.
The tail might be on *him,* with no connection to the Stick,
and that in turn could mean that someone wanted Fowler put away.

The punks from Dorsey Park? Some trigger-happy
losers from an ancient case?

Rodriguez?

Fowler led them to North River Drive, the fast lane,
running toward a 45-degree dead end where Northwest
Twentieth and Northwest Twenty-seventh met above the

river west of Curtis Park. The tail car was keeping pace and even gaining on him now, its driver shifting lanes to come up on his right.

He drifted the Camaro over, blocking them, and reached inside his jacket for the Glock 17 automatic, which he set down on the empty shotgun seat beside him with the safety off. A live round in the chamber gave him eighteen chances if it came to shooting, and he wouldn't be taken out the first thing off the bat.

He checked the rearview mirror, saw a muzzle-flash behind the glaring headlights and dropped in his seat as shotgun pellets salted the Camaro's tail. A cherry paint job shot to hell.

''Goddamn it!''

Fowler stood on the accelerator, running for it, but the dark sedan kept pace, the headlights veering back and forth to try and pass him on either side where they could get a decent shot. He fishtailed, losing some of his acceleration in the process, but he couldn't block them off forever.

Coming up beside him on his left, the chase car nudged him with a fender, near the left rear wheel. He kept it on the road by veering back and hitting them a solid broadside, wincing at the damage he could picture in his mind.

Forget it, he told himself. You can always spring for bodywork if you're alive.

The heavier chase car was hanging tough, and another shotgun blast exploded through the left rear window, spraying the interior with pebbled glass.

Too close.

He palmed the Glock and squeezed off three quick shots without really aiming. He'd be lucky if he hit the car, much less the men inside. It served to startle them, as though they'd thought they were up against an unarmed man, and the chase car fell back a length before the driver found his nerve.

He saw them coming in the mirror, muzzle-flash and headlights, buckshot raking claw marks on the driver's door. At least one pellet burrowed through and hit the dash, miraculously missing Fowler as he twisted in his seat.

This time, figuring he didn't have much to lose, he turned around to aim, his left hand steady on the steering wheel. The gunner was behind him, out of range, but Fowler glimpsed the driver as a chunky silhouette behind the windshield and squeezed off two rounds that chipped the glass and made his adversary hit the breaks again.

The dead end was coming up, and Fowler had to make a choice—due east on Twentieth past Curtis Park, or south on Twenty-seventh, under the expressway toward the Tamiami Trail. If he went south as far as Flagler, hung a left, he stood a decent chance of losing them in traffic. Failing that, a few more miles and he could lead them to the Federal Building, see if that amused the bastards. Maybe take a left off Flagler onto Second Street and drop them off at Metro-Dade instead.

In fact his adversaries stole the choice away from Fowler with a lucky shot that blew his left front tire. He fought the skid one-handed for a moment, giving up the pistol as he tried to keep it on the road, but there was no way he could save the game at close to eighty miles an hour. His brakes locked up with a screaming of rubber, and another shotgun blast came through the window, making Fowler duck to keep from splattering the dashboard with his brains.

He hit the curb and felt the undercarriage snag for just a heartbeat, freed up as the muffler ripped away. A guardrail kept the car from rolling—saved his life, in fact, considering the steep drop to the riverbed—but Fowler's door was crumpled shut and wedged against the rail.

He found the Glock and lunged across the console, cursing as the gear shift jabbed him in the groin. The rider's door was functional, and Fowler tumbled out headfirst, his knees and elbows scuffing gravel as he fell.

The chase car overshot and had to double back, the brake lights winking at him as he lurched around in back of the Camaro, crouching so the trunk would give him something in the way of cover when they came. He braced the automatic in a firm two-handed grip, his elbows planted on the trunk lid, and waited for them to come and get him.

From a block away, he saw the chase car slowing, angling for another shot, the gunner craning out to draw a bead. The light was bad, and they were almost out of range, but Fowler took his shot. Thirteen of them, in fact, spent brass dancing over the Camaro's trunk.

He heard a couple of the rounds strike metal, probably a fender or the grille, before the wheelman put it in reverse and got the hell away from there. Too far away to read his license plate, the yellow bastard running east on Twentieth and out of sight.

He pocketed the empty magazine and slipped a fresh one in before he rose on shaky legs. It didn't figure they would try another pass, but you could never tell.

His wheels were trashed—not totaled, necessarily, but close enough—and he would have to find a telephone ASAP. If it was Dorsey Park, he had to tip off Enriquez before another team came knocking at his door.

And if it wasn't Dorsey Park . . . then, what?

A question begging answers that he did not have.

He slipped the Glock inside his waistband, fetched his keys from the car out of habit and started south on Twenty-seventh, looking for a phone.

He would call Enriquez first, then Rick the Stick. If both were safe and sound, there would be ample time to scout the other possibilities.

A telephone, then wheels.

And he would have to find himself a dealer who could sing.

5

Osvaldo Arias was thankful every day for the insipid moron who designed the U.S. immigration laws. Instead of keeping certain elements out, the patchwork legislation seemed designed to draw them *in,* a shining lure for renegades and losers from around the world. It seemed that people who were having problems in their native land, especially with the courts and the police, were encouraged to make tracks for the United States and start all over in the golden Land of Opportunity. For those fleeing from a communist regime, it was so much the better; all would be forgiven, with the gates thrown open wide.

Of course, it wasn't *quite* that simple, but it worked out well enough for Arias, an inmate serving time for rape and robbery in one of Cuba's stinking jails when Castro opened up the port of Mariel to emigrants in April 1980. After twenty years of hard-line tactics had failed to crush dissent or stifle foreign criticism, Castro finally announced that anyone dissatisfied with his progressive revolution was at liberty to leave.

There was, however, one small catch.

As the mosquito fleet of private craft from southern Florida arrived at Mariel, the word came down from soldiers standing watch. For every friend or relative retrieved, each skipper was required to take at least three strangers on his boat, no questions asked—125,000 souls altogether, before the exodus was done.

It took a while for Immigration and the Customs men to realize Fidel was cleaning out his jails and mental in-

stitutions at America's expense. By that time, thousands
of convicted felons and unbalanced individuals were safe
in the United States, all pleading for political asylum, and
the port of Mariel was closed again.

In time the human tide dispersed across the landscape, but a fair percentage of the new arrivals lingered
in Miami, mixing naturally with the established residents of Little Havana. The impact of their presence was
immediately felt, as drug-related homicides increased by
sixty-two percent before year's end, with the police solution rate for same declining to an all-time record low of
thirty-three percent.

Miami had become the nation's murder capital, and
there were those who swore they could almost hear the
mocking laughter, ninety miles off-shore.

As for Osvaldo Arias, he wasn't laughing. There was
too damned much to do, adjusting to a brand-new cul-
ture where the laws were seemingly concocted to protect
the guilty. It was a refreshing change, and Arias took full
advantage of his new environment, building up a stake
through strong-arm robberies, investing in a small-scale
shipment of cocaine that turned a tidy profit on the
street.

The rest was history.

Currently Osvaldo was a citizen of the United States,
with four arrests and no convictions on his record in Miami. Nearly twenty-seven months had passed since he
had seen the inside of a jail, except for visiting a couple
of his cronies when they went away. He was a man of
substance, with a not so modest income, proud of what
he had achieved the past ten years.

There had been challenges along the way, of course; a
new land testing new arrivals, weeding out the small fry
and selecting those who made the grade. Osvaldo learned
to deal with the American police and high-priced law-

yers, covert arms suppliers, the Colombians who held a virtual monopoly on distribution of cocaine. He dealt with competition as the need arose and chalked up seven murders by the time he raised his hand and swore an oath of loyalty to the Stars and Stripes. The past five years or so, there had been ten or fifteen others. He was losing count and did not really care, as long as money kept flowing in.

Which brought Jorge Rodriguez back to mind, and a sour expression tugged at the corners of Osvaldo's mouth.

The slick Colombian had been a valued source at first, but times were changing for the worse around Miami. In the past few months, Rodriguez had been turning up the heat on former clients, fielding teams of gunmen and corrupt police to keep the pressure on, diverting shipments and harassing—sometimes killing—independent dealers on the street. The raids went down like clockwork, with Rodriguez waiting in the wings to offer his assistance selling them ''insurance'' with the premiums established on a sliding scale of thirty-five to fifty-five percent per month, depending on the target's scope of operations.

Arias had managed to resist for several weeks, a skirmish here and there with minor casualties, until the night he was ''arrested'' at his favorite nightclub by a team of uniformed police. Instead of taking him to jail, they drove Osvaldo to a warehouse fronting Biscayne Bay and introduced him to the officer in charge. Osvaldo's seven-hundred-dollar suit was sliced away with razors, and he stood before them naked, trying not to tremble, as their spokesman briefed him on the new rules of survival in Miami.

He had gone in cracking wise, defiant in the face of almost certain death, until the man in charge explained that no one meant to harm a wavy hair on poor Osvaldo's head. The tickle of a razor blade against his scrotum made the point, and Arias acquired a silent partner in the business he had built from scratch.

These days he walked the streets in relative security, "protected" by Rodriguez and the same police who swore an oath to put him out of business in Miami. Sometimes Osvaldo even left his retinue of private bodyguards at home.

And it only cost him a forty-sixty split...together with his pride.

This evening, Arias was flying solo and enjoying it, still mindful of the risk from smaller independent operators, fairly confident that his association with Rodriguez and his own ferocious reputation should be adequate to keep him safe. In any case, he savored risk these days, recapturing a measure of the heady feeling from his early days around Miami when he had to fight for every inch of ground.

It made Osvaldo feel alive.

The whorehouse on Alhambra, in Coral Gables, catered to a small, exclusive clientele. No drop-ins were permitted, and the list of regulars included politicians, jurists, heavy dealers and a scattering of media celebrities. You booked a party in advance and paid up front, with satisfaction guaranteed for every taste.

Tonight Osvaldo had a taste for something young and fresh. Not necessarily a virgin—where the hell could anybody dig one up, these days?—but close enough. A tender morsel that would make him feel alive, restore a measure of the manhood he had grudgingly surrendered in a warehouse by the bay.

Emerging from the elevator in the underground garage of his apartment building, Arias took time to glance around him, checking out the shadows for potential ene-

mies. Old habits never really died, like carrying the Smith
& Wesson automatic in his belt, the hammer pressed
against his spine. How long since he himself had pulled
the trigger on a man?

Too long.

He had three cars on hand, paid extra for the parking
spaces, and tonight he felt like driving the Corvette. It
was a sex machine, virility on wheels, and he would get a
lift from listening to all that power throbbing underneath the hood.

Already feeling better, Arias moved past the Cadillac
Allante and the BMW, homing in on the Corvette con-
vertible. He had the keys in hand, was whistling softly to
himself, when someone stepped in close behind him and
the muzzle of a handgun pressed against the angle of his
jaw.

"Be smart, Osvaldo."

He stood silently as the gunner's free hand slid inside
his jacket, found the automatic in his belt and worked it
free. The search was quick and thoroughly professional.

"No boys, tonight?"

"I'm on my own."

"That's nice," the gunman said. "Let's take a ride."

HE CUFFED Osvaldo's hands behind him, slapped a strip
of duct tape on his mouth and put him on the floor behind the driver's seat. The Smith & Wesson went into his
glove compartment for a backup piece in case he needed
one.

So far, so good.

The drive to Medley, through Hialeah and Miami
Springs, used up half an hour. Fowler knew Osvaldo's
people would be looking for him pretty soon, but finding him was something else. They still had time, and he
was not inclined to rush.

He parked the rental Ford along a gravel track that circled an expansive reservoir, lush cattails sprouting on the bank as if the lake were natural and not man-made.

It didn't make a bit of difference either way tonight, as long as it was deep.

He dragged Osvaldo out and got the dealer on his feet, beside the car. The duct tape made a ripping sound, and Osvaldo cursed at the sudden pain.

"You swim?"

The dealer blinked and glanced around him at the cattails, the flat expanse of water shining like a plain of tinted glass.

"Say what?"

"I asked you if you swim. It's yes or no, Osvaldo."

"Sí."

"That's fine."

"I know you?"

"Absolutely. I'm the guy's about to help you set a record."

"¿Qué?"

"It's perfectly legitimate, I promise you. I'm taking notes and everything."

"What kind of record?" The man was looking nervous now, as if he could see it coming.

Fowler cracked a smile. "The longest underwater swim without an Aqua-lung. It's in the bag."

"You crazy, man!"

"Don't let it worry you. It hardly bothers me at all."

He shoved Osvaldo toward the reservoir, the dealer dragging ass until he tapped the muzzle of the Glock against his skull.

"Somebody paying you for this?"

"I volunteered."

Osvaldo wasn't buying it. "You tell me what they offer you, I double it."

"A little to your left, there. You can see a path, down through the reeds."

"I triple it! Just name your price, okay?"

"It goes to show you how some people get things wrong. I heard you were the type hangs on a dollar tight enough to make old Georgie bleed."

"You're making a mistake."

"No, I believe it's deep enough right here."

"I got connections, like, you know?"

"That's what I heard."

"The kind of people you don't want to piss them off."

"I'll take my chances. Here we go."

The muddy bank had leveled off. In front of them the water was a sheet of solid ebony.

"How much you want? To call it off?"

"Wade out right there—I figure you can make it five, six strides before the water hits your waist. From there, it drops off pretty quick."

"My hands."

"Don't mind the cuffs. I've got another pair at home."

"You gonna have to shoot me first."

"Okay."

He raised the Glock and fired a round across Osvaldo's shoulder, past his ear. The dealer jumped and wet himself, a dark stain spreading at his crotch.

"Hold still, for Christ's sake. That's twelve cents you cost me."

"Wait! Who *are* you?"

"I'm your swimming coach. I thought we had that squared away."

"There must be *something* I can do."

"Well, since you put it that way..."

"Sure, I knew it."

"Information."

"What?"

"I'll start. You're dealing with Rodriguez, even though you'd rather not. He muscled in your business, and you're not amused. The punch line is, he's using cops for muscle on the street."

"I didn't hear you ask a question."

"Names," said Fowler. "Give the bluesuits up and you can walk home. Otherwise you swim."

"What kind of crazy fucking deal—"

The next round whispered past the dealer's face and raised a water spout behind him in the reservoir.

"I'm getting tired of this, Osvaldo."

"Names you want? What makes you think these fuckers introduce themselves?"

"A man like you, with such connections, something tells me you could ask around."

"It's possible I might've got the honcho's name."

"I'm listening."

"Thing is, I don't know who I'm talking to. It gets around I gave you names, and pretty soon Rodriguez wants to take me for a ride."

"I guess you'll have to trust me there."

"I only got the one name anyhow."

"You said that."

"Just the bum in charge, you understand? I figure what the hell, the other guys are taking orders, right?"

"You're wasting time."

"Lieutenant Steele. Guy spells it with an *e* like, on the end. His first name's Ervin."

"Cute."

"That's all, I swear."

"You met this joker face-to-face?"

"One time." Osvaldo scowled, remembering, his face gone hard. "You want to kill the motherfucker, it's all right with me."

"Sounds like you fellas didn't hit it off."

"Supposed to be a cop, and here he's stealing from a working man. What kind of law is that?"

"Beats me, Osvaldo. Myself, I'm in favor of the firing squad, where pushers are concerned."

"Hey, I'm a businessman, okay? If everybody wanted Tootsie Rolls the way they want a little candy for the nose, I'd have a chocolate shop. It's how things are."

"How much have you been paying to Rodriguez?"

"What?"

"Osvaldo." He brought up the Glock, so it was level with his sweaty face.

"We make a sixty-forty split."

"Who gets the sixty?"

"I do, what you think?"

"I wouldn't be surprised if Rodriguez asked for a cost-of-living raise before too long."

"You want to be my agent now or what?"

"No thanks. How many cops does Steele have working for him on the shakedowns?"

"How the hell should I know?"

"Take a guess."

"First time I met him, there was three. Now that I think about it, him and those three are the only ones I ever saw."

"No names?"

"I answered that already, didn't I?"

"You should be hoping I believe you."

"Either way. You want, I can make up some names."

"Don't bother."

"Are we finished now?"

"Not quite. I let you walk, your boys may have some questions. Where you've been and all."

"So fuck 'em. I don't have to tell them anything. They work for me."

"Could be you'll feel like picking up the phone and talking to Rodriguez, telling him about our little chat."

"You think so? Like I need more trouble in my life the way it is. I call him up and say some guy I never seen before came out of nowhere, took me for a ride and made me spill my guts. I'm sure."

"You put it that way, maybe I don't have to waste you after all."

"I get a vote? How 'bout you drop me off downtown somewhere, and I can take a taxi home. Hop in the 'Vette and go about my business like we never met. I'm running late, but what the hell."

"You'll have to hitch, Osvaldo. Sorry, but I haven't got the time to play chauffeur."

"About these cuffs...?"

"I guess you'd better turn around."

The dealer hesitated, staring at the gun in Fowler's hand. "You're being straight now, right?"

"No sweat. I'd let you watch if I had anything in mind."

"Okay."

He turned around, and Fowler set the pistol's safety, stepping forward as he swung the butt against Osvaldo's skull, behind one ear. The dealer grunted like a pig and toppled forward in the reeds.

His face was in the muck, and Fowler dragged him back a yard or so to let him breathe. Unfastening the cuffs was easy, and he left Osvaldo there to sleep it off. No snakes or alligators in the reservoir, but the mosquitos had to eat like everybody else.

Returning to Miami proper on the Okeechobee Road, he thought about Lieutenant Ervin Steele. The name was not familiar from his time at Metro-Dade, but there was no reason why it should be, after nine years off the job.

It didn't follow automatically that Steele was Keegan's target, either, but at least it was a place to start.

With names in hand, he could begin to chart a paper trail between Rodriguez and the officer in question, locate some bank accounts, perhaps a bit of real estate. It would require time to finger Steele's accomplices, but he would nail them all before he wrapped it up.

He owed Glen Keegan that much, anyway.

He also owed it to himself.

6

"You *missed* him?"

Facing Ervin Steele across a littered desk, Frank Meadows shook his head emphatically. "*I* didn't miss the bastard, *Skirvin* missed him. *I* was driving, like I told you."

The lieutenant felt his cheeks flush crimson underneath a cultivated tan. He glared at Meadows for a moment, swallowing the urge to reach across his desk and slap the sergeant's face or throttle him.

"You think I care who pulled the trigger, Frank? Is that your fantasy? I give you simple work to do, and you come back with nothing, blaming someone else."

"I wouldn't call it simple work, Lieutenant. The guy was shooting back, you know?"

"The point is, *you* were shooting first. You had the numbers, and you were supposed to take him by surprise. I should be sitting here and reading his obituary now, instead of hearing how you fucked it up."

"He made us right away. We would've had to waste him in the parking lot before he drove away, and there were too damned many witnesses. I'm telling you, the guy's a shark."

"I hear you saying you can't handle him?"

Frank Meadows stiffened in his straight-backed chair. "Another chance, that's all. The fucker's good as dead."

"No further moves until I give the word," Steele told him, glaring daggers. "Understood?"

"I hear you."

"When you talk to Skirvin, tell him I expect to see him on the firing range at least an hour for the next five days."

"Okay. What's shaking with Rodriguez?"

Steele resented being questioned by subordinates, but he restrained himself from lashing out. "We've got a meet this afternoon. New work, I wouldn't be surprised."

"All right. You need a backup going in?"

"No sweat."

"You're telling me you trust Rodriguez now?"

"We understand each other, Frank. He's got no call to make a move on me. Best part, he knows what happens if he does."

"Okay, you say so."

"Trust me, Sergeant," Steele said, using rank to put the other in his place. "You talk to Skirvin. I'll take care of business on the other end."

"Yes, *sir*."

Meadows looked a little peevish as he left, and that was fine. Lieutenant Ervin Steele believed in keeping a strategic distance from subordinates, regardless of the enterprise, and dealing with Jorge Rodriguez on the side had only emphasized his need to exercise authority. If Meadows and the others started thinking they were friends rather than soldiers in a private war, then they might begin to challenge his authority, start thinking for themselves.

Last night was bad enough, when they appeared to follow orders. It wasn't the first time they had screwed a contract up to some extent, but at least they had never let the target walk before.

If anything, it usually went the other way. Send Meadows, Hicks and Skirvin out to smoke a guy, and you stood a decent chance of having three, four corpses on your hands before they finished up. Potential witnesses, of course, and thus expendable. Steele would not fault his men for covering their tracks.

The Fowler tag was life insurance... or should have been, before his shooters fucked it up. It didn't take a Sherlock Holmes to figure out the Fed would start to nose around his one-time partner's death, and there was heat enough around Rodriguez as it was without a personal vendetta kicking in. If they could pick him off before he got a decent start on making Keegan's death a federal case, they would be points ahead. The brass at DEA would look to Fowler's caseload for potential suspects and find plenty they could choose from in the absence of conclusive evidence.

But he was still alive.

That made it tricky, with the odds of an arrest increased on each attempt, but they were in too deep to simply let it slide. If necessary, Steele would do the job himself, make sure it got done right.

Twelve years with Metro-Dade, and the one thing Ervin Steele had never been accused of by his friends *or* by his enemies was laziness. He never did a job halfway or left unsightly loose ends dangling in the breeze. You gave a job to Steele, he handled everything.

It was a reputation he had carried straight from the academy. He was a can-do kind of guy who saved his training partner's life the third week he was on the streets. No looking back from there.

In retrospect, Steele told himself that it had been a fluke. Okay, *lucky* fluke. His first month in the black-and-white, Steele drew the graveyard shift in Overtown, the second-toughest ghetto in Miami. Vincent Esposito was his partner, eight years on the job and tough as nails. He didn't carry any special grudge against the blacks, but if they stepped across that line, he treated them like any other asshole on the wrong side of the law.

The night in question was a muggy Saturday. They passed an all-night liquor store and caught a glimpse of guns inside, two youngbloods ripping off the night man for a couple of hundred bucks and slapping him around because he didn't have the combination to the safe.

Steele called it in, armed robbery in progress, satisfied to wait for backup on the street. His partner saw it differently, afraid the two young punks might waste their victim on a whim or wriggle out the back while they sat waiting for the cavalry. He took the unit's 12-gauge and cut down a narrow alley that circled around back, leaving Steele out front with orders to remain in place.

There was no hint of the sirens yet when Steele observed the two armed subjects bailing out. The back door, right. He wasn't even thinking as he ran across the street and through the swinging doors, his fingers almost numb the way he gripped his blue-steel Colt. A burst of gunfire out in back, and Steele kept going, getting there in time to see his partner on the ground, one of the youngbloods standing over him and lining up the coup de grace.

The rest of it got jumbled in his mind these days, like film clips from a movie that you've seen a hundred times and are still not exactly sure about. He killed them both, that much was clear—the commendation told him so— but mostly he remembered noise and muzzle-flashes, jerky images like something from a two-bit peep show where the crank is turned by hand.

There was a fair amount of heat, the dead guys being black, but Steele was cleared by IAD, the shooting board, the coroner's report. The chief caught flak for keeping him in Overtown another month or so, but it was something that he had to do. If people get the notion they can bulldoze law and order with a few chaotic demonstrations in the street, society begins to come apart.

And that was what had happened in Miami on a different level. Steele was not concerned with placing blame—the Cubans, blacks, Colombians, the liberals—for what was going down around him, happening before his very eyes while he was powerless to intervene. He learned that wasting strong-arm robbers earned you praise, while generating heat for well-connected dealers had the opposite effect. Forget that money talked around Miami, and a guy could finish up his twenty years in Overtown a human target every time he hit the street.

Promotion was not difficult for Ervin Steele. He had a good head on his shoulders, commendations in his file, the reputation of a stand-up guy who took no shit. His third year on the job, he took the sergeant's test and passed with flying colors, got his stripes that fall and tested for lieutenant two years later. The assignment to Narcotics was a plum, despite the risks involved. Before he transferred in from Homicide, Steele knew that there was major money on the table. He had learned the practical realities of law and order in Miami, making up his mind that it was time to claim his share.

And then some.

Milking independent dealers was the easy part. They lived and stayed in business by the sufferance of cops like Steele, who took their cash and hassled them enough to satisfy appearances, providing tip-offs when a major push was underway. Connecting with the big cartels was something else. You didn't go to them; they came to you.

Just the way Jorge Rodriguez came to Ervin Steele eighteen months ago.

The game was rather different than his normal action on the streets. Instead of simply being paid to look the other way, Steele was expected to participate, recruit a handful of subordinates.

The latter part was easy in Narcotics: half the street cops stood with their hands out, while the other half kept shoveling against the tide. The trick was to pick just the right recruits and trust them to keep their mouths shut as they went along. The wrong word, anywhere along the line, and they were history. A cell upstate at best. At worst...

But it was easy, once the team got squared away. They mostly squeezed the independent dealers like before, but with a twist. Instead of being satisfied with regular protection payments, their employer wanted to achieve a stranglehold on traffic in Miami and environs. His competitors were actively discouraged by a combination of techniques: selective confiscation of their product; numerous arrests; a beating now and then. If they were still defiant, stricter measures were applied. It only took a few deaths in the trade before word got around.

Still, working for Rodriguez was a tightrope act of sorts. One slip could be the last, no safety net below to break the fall. If any one of them was busted, he would have to take the fall alone or risk reprisals coming down on both sides of the law.

And now, with Jackson Fowler, they had slipped. The contract had been organized on Steele's initiative, and they had blown it. There was no way it could be dressed up and called a success.

Rodriguez would have heard by now. The guy heard everything, reacting swiftly when an incident appeared to jeopardize his empire. He was not averse to dusting cops, but it would always be a last resort. Steele thought he had a decent chance of living through the night, provided he was humble and admitted his mistakes, no lame excuses like his gunner couldn't shoot straight in the dark. Sincerity—or its facsimile—was paramount in dealing with the man.

But he would take along his lucky Bren Ten automatic, just in case.

It never hurt to be prepared.

JORGE LUIS RODRIGUEZ trusted no one—and corrupt policemen least of all. They were like prostitutes, except that women working on the streets made no pretense of virtue while they plied their trade. A dirty cop, by definition, was a two-faced animal who served the highest bidder, selling out himself and his oath of office for the cash in hand.

Rodriguez had no quarrel with greed, as such. It made the world go round, and every human being on the planet had a price. The avarice displayed by some policemen confirmed his view of man in general and specifically the deputized authorities. They cared no more about the public than Rodriguez did, each badge intent on looking out for number one.

There were occasional exceptions to the rule, of course. A handful of crusaders, bent on lying to the world at large and to themselves, denying their attraction to the sweet life, working overtime to prove their masculinity by challenging the odds. It made them feel like holy martyrs, cleaning up a town that never had been—never would be—clean.

The truth was that Miami did not *want* a cleanup. Never mind the politicians' speeches, headlines warning of a plague that must be fought with every instrument at hand. If the illicit drug trade dried up overnight, those politicians would be stricken dumb, compelled to scramble for another issue that would net them votes. Reporters would be out of work; the fire-and-brimstone ministers, who never quite had nerve enough to name

Rodriguez from their pulpits, would be begging quarters on the street.

Jorge Rodriguez viewed the cocaine traffic as a service industry. Americans were hungry for the powder from his native Medellín, and he supplied it . . . at a healthy price. He also doubled as a kind of modern bogeyman, a figure variously used to frighten wayward children, boost the local television ratings and seduce the voters into casting ballots for the latest law-and-order candidates.

In fact, Rodriguez was a lot like God. If he did not exist, Miami's power structure would have to dream him up.

But even bogeymen pay dues.

One cost of doing business in Miami was the absolute necessity of dealing with police, from beat cops to the brass hats in command. Rodriguez hated the facade of holier-than-thou respectability they shared in common, holding out their hands for cash as if the money *he* had earned was somehow theirs by right. Still, the police were necessary in their way.

They helped Rodriguez to preserve appearances.

And some of them were helpful when he had a spot of dirty work to do.

Lieutenant Ervin Steele was one of those, an officer who got things done on time, according to his orders. His subordinates enjoyed their work—too much, at times— but violent men were useful in their proper place.

Jorge Rodriguez was a violent man himself. Or had been, once upon a time, when he was living on the streets of Medellín and scratching for a place in the narcotics trade. He found that place behind a gun, and carried out a dozen murders, give or take, before he reached the legal voting age. His reputation as a killer served him well in later years, reminding his competitors and would-be traitors in his own cartel of the potential risks involved in challenging a self-made man.

These days Rodriguez had an army at his beck and call, young men to serve at his command. Aside from the prestige, it helped protect him from arrest, his soldiers well aware of what would happen if they ended up in jail and spilled their guts.

The meet with Ervin Steele posed a problem, but Rodriguez always dealt from strength with his employees. Steele had stepped outside the bounds of his authority, and some response was mandatory to prevent a repetition of the incident.

Next time the narcs from Metro-Dade set out to kill a fellow officer, they would be acting under orders from the man who paid the larger of their separate salaries.

Security was paramount when meeting with his contacts on the force, and Rodriguez took pains to guard against discovery. He knew that federal watchdogs from assorted agencies maintained surveillance on his every move, but he had ways of shaking them when there was business to be done. Tonight he sent the limo out ahead of time to draw them out, then waited for an hour prior to hiding in the back seat of a cheap sedan, one of his gunmen at the wheel. If anyone remained on guard outside his house, they would report only a member of the staff departing alone for an evening on the town.

His destination was a small but stylish restaurant in Hallandale, close by the dog track. Parking in the rear, his soldier verified that they had not been followed, then proceeded to wait while Rodriguez used his private entrance to a second-story office suite above the dining room. He had been waiting twenty minutes when a bouncer from the restaurant delivered Ervin Steele.

"Sit down."

No rank, no name. Rodriguez took command immediately, letting his displeasure show. Steele found himself a chair and dragged it closer to the desk. His eyes were shifty, undermining his show of curiosity about the summons.

Even as he spoke, Steele knew that his all-innocent approach was a feeble sham. "So, what's up?"

Rodriguez kept his face devoid of expression. "Did someone ask you to eliminate a Fed?"

"This Fowler guy, you mean? I had to use my own initiative on that."

"Explain."

"The guy was Keegan's partner, way back when. I guess he got a better offer from the DEA or something. Anyway, the word is that they kept in touch."

"So what?"

"So Fowler, from what I hear around the job, is not a live-and-let-live kind of guy. He holds a grudge, and someone stepping on his buddy is the kind of thing might set him off. On top of that, I figure Keegan may have told him something, if he thought he couldn't talk around the shop."

"And *you* decided he should die."

"That's right. Insurance, like."

"Assuming you were right, what happened?"

"Well..."

"The truth."

"You think I came up here to lie?"

"You came because I called you. You had no choice."

A smudge of angry color tinged Steele's face. He didn't like reminders of his own subordinate position in the scheme of things.

"I sent two guys, but Fowler saw them coming. That's what *they* say, anyhow. They fucked it up and missed the first shot, so Fowler started blasting, then wrecked his car. They didn't want to take a chance on witnesses."

"They weren't seen?"

Steele shook his head. "They stole a car and dumped it afterward. I took a squint at Fowler's statement down at Homicide this morning. His descriptions aren't worth shit."

"But you've alerted him."

"To what? He's working two, three cases any given day. There's men he busted, going back ten years or more, who'd like to see him dead. He's nowhere."

"With his partner freshly killed, you don't believe he'll look for a connection?"

Steele dismissed the danger with a shrug. "*What* connection? Besides, he won't have time to look for anything—my people got another shot lined up."

"Correction. You will *not* attempt to follow through unless I order it."

"Hey, now, we let him walk—"

Rodriguez brought his fist down on the desktop, hard enough to coax a soft ping from the telephone. Steele shut his mouth and waited, frozen in his chair.

"You don't get paid to think," Rodriguez snapped. "Instead of taking Fowler on and blowing it, you should have found out what he's working on, how much he knows. Who was he talking to last night?"

"We're checking that right now."

"That's *all* you check unless I tell you otherwise. ¿Comprende?"

"Sure. Okay." Steele's answer was reluctant, but he'd given in because he had no choice. Then he asked, "Suppose it *is* connected?"

"Then we'll know about it soon enough."

"My ass is riding on the line, you know."

"Remember that the next time you begin to use initiative."

Steele had another comment ready, but he wisely reconsidered. "Are we done?"

Rodriguez watched him sweat it out a moment longer, finally putting on a smile devoid of warmth.

"You'll keep in touch?"

"First thing I hear."

"Tomorrow."

Agreement was given grudgingly. "Okay."

Rodriguez watched him go, indifferent to his anger and embarrassment. The dealer had more pressing matters on his mind just then . . . like coping with a federal agent on the eve of pulling down his biggest coup in years.

If Steele had queered the action, he would pay for his mistake in blood, regardless of his badge and rank.

But first, the Fed.

Jack Fowler might not know it, but his time was running out. Whatever Steele's investigation finally disclosed, Fowler was as good as dead.

It was the only way Jorge Rodriguez knew to play the game.

7

Rudy Stano shuffled the computer printouts on his desk and rocked back in his swivel chair to face Jack Fowler. "Let me have the *Reader's Digest* version, will you?"

"Right." He went ahead without consulting any notes: the information was burned into his brain. "Rodriguez and the good lieutenant both do all their banking in Miami out of Bay Shores Federal Savings...which by some coincidence is partly owned by the Rodriguez family."

"Specifics?"

"Four, five years ago, Rodriguez started shopping for a place to keep his money safe, once it's been laundered off the coast. He's not concerned about a holdup, but he hates the IRS."

"I can imagine."

"Anyway, he figured it would be a bonus if he had a bank where he controlled the officers in charge, so they could tip him off about investigations, audits, seizures—little things like that."

"Go on." The words reached Fowler through a cloud of fresh cigar smoke as Stano lighted up his second Cuban of the day.

"By spring of '87, Jorge and a couple of his trusted aides had managed to accumulate some fifty-two percent of voting stock in Bay Shore Federal, purchased on the open market. Nothing shady on the deal, per se, except for their intentions once the deal went through."

"And now they hold the strings?"

"Affirmative. Rodriguez and his people deal primarily with Bay Shore Federal for their savings, checking, safe-deposit boxes, business loans—you name it. As it happens, so does one Lieutenant Ervin Steele.''

"So what? We can't go into court with a coincidence like that.''

"Agreed. But Steele has *two* accounts at Bay Shore Federal, under different names. He also got a brand-new house financed at three points under prime. The past two years he's taken out three major loans that never seem to get repaid.''

"The IRS is on to this?''

"They're playing wait-and-see. Don't ask me why.''

"And the other cops you're looking for?''

"Still looking, but I'll give you odds they turn up banking with Rodriguez when we get the names.''

"No bet.'' The section chief was frowning through a veil of smoke. "We still need more to work on. Otherwise I'd say the way to go is give it to the tax boys, try to light a fire that way.''

"There's more,'' said Fowler.

"So?''

"Rodriguez and his stooges don't just bank together in Miami. They've been washing millions out of Nassau, export from the States to any one of two, three friendly banks, then bring it back as 'loans' to Bay Shore Federal.''

"And the loans?''

"When they're repaid at all, drug money covers it, clean cash comes back.''

"If you can make that stick ....''

"Then we can seize the stateside bank accounts. I'm way ahead of you. And there's a kicker.''

"Yeah?''

"Three guesses which lieutenant out of Metro-Dade Narcotics has been dealing with a certain bank in Nassau for the past eleven months.''

"Okay, we're getting there," said Stano, "but we still need someone who can put it together on the witness stand. The seizures have to pass inspection, and Rodriguez won't be sitting on his hands, not with all the lawyers he's got marking time."

"I'm thinking that maybe I should make a run to Nassau."

"Working on your tan?"

"I always liked the sun."

"You're jumping in a different game down there, with Pindling's crowd. You can forget about that 'excellent cooperation' bullshit in the D.C. press release. The Mob, in one form or another, has been running Nassau since the Lansky team helped put the the native government in power back in '67. The prime minister himself averages a half-million dollars per year in loans and gifts from shady characters, and that's only the tip of the iceberg, half a million they don't try to hide. You tell me Rodriguez has buddies in Nassau, and I say what else is new?"

"I'm hoping the country office can put me in touch with a viable source," Fowler said. "You want a witness, affidavits, and we'll need someone in the islands to support a chain of evidence."

"Why not let Nassau cover it?"

"They're overloaded as it is. Besides, I've got the motivation."

"Which reminds me," Stano said, "I talked to the M.E. last night."

"I'm listening."

"Keegan had four bullet wounds. Three in the left hip and abdomen were all 9-mm parabellum with a right-hand twist. Could be an SMG or any one of half a dozen automatics."

"That leaves one."

"The head shot killed him, Jack, 10-mm semiauto. Narrows down your choices to the Brens, the Parker, or Colt's Delta Elite. Better odds for a match if they ever come up with the piece."

"Is Homicide in touch with ATF?"

"I wouldn't be surprised. A cop goes down like that, they beat the bushes pretty good. Of course, the rumor mill's been working overtime."

"I heard."

Glen Keegan's manner of death—off duty, dressed in black and painted up for war, shot execution-style—had been a natural for gossipmongers both in and out of the department. By the time the undertakers planted Keegan, word had trickled down suggesting *he* was dirty, working for some unnamed local dealer on the side. The cops who knew him shrugged it off or put the gossips in their place, but there were many others—even in Narcotics—who had never met the man. Bad news spreads fast, and ugly rumors have a tendency to stick.

"It's like your basic needle in the haystack, anyway," said Stano. "Ever since they had Don Johnson use the Bren Ten on *Miami Vice,* you've got a whole new market opened up. Remember Dirty Harry's Smith & Wesson Model 29? For three, four years, you couldn't keep 'em in the stores at any price. Today you pick one up without a six-month wait or taking out a second mortgage on your house. Times change."

"In other words, I shouldn't hold my breath."

"You never looked that great in blue."

"No progress on the hit car from the other night?"

"Forget about the fingerprints. They wiped it clean. And it was hot, of course. The owner runs a string of Laundromats in Miramar. Got up that morning and the car was gone. No obvious connection with Rodriguez, but he's mad as hell about the paint job."

"Tough shit."

"That's what I like, compassion for the average citizen."

"I'll cry when I get back from Nassau, if I have the time."

"You're going when, tomorrow?"

"Or the next day if I get hung up. There's still a couple things I need to tidy up. Loose ends."

"See Teddy Jakes when you get in. I'll tell him to expect a call, and you can run the details down yourself."

"Okay."

He rose to leave, and Stano came around the desk to face him.

"Watch your ass in Nassau, Jack. We've got an office on the island, but it doesn't mean we're in control. To tell you the truth, it doesn't even mean we know what's going on."

"That's off the record, I assume."

"Damn right. Officially, we're one big happy family, allied in the holy war on drugs."

"I'll watch it."

"Do that, will you? Lots of sun in Nassau, Jack. I wouldn't want to see you burned."

HE WATCHED the rearview mirror for a tail on Highway 1, came up with nothing by the time he reached Le Jeune and headed south. No place to park in front of Molly Keegan's house on Poinciana, so he left the rental two doors down and doubled back. She answered Fowler's knock in faded jeans, a Metro T-shirt, sandals and a surprised expression.

"Jack."

"I'm going out of town tomorrow, maybe Wednesday, and I thought I'd see if there was anything you need before I go."

"Come in." She held the screen door open for him, then latched it after he was safe inside. "Vacation?"

"Business. Listen, if I'm interrupting anything . . ."

"Please, do. I've had this overwhelming urge to clean the house, since . . . well, the past few days. I've done the whole place, twice I think it is. I need a break."

"How's Tommy?"

"Back in school. I would have let him slide another day or two, but he was getting jumpy, cooped up in the house. Can't say I blame him. Coffee?"

"Only if it's made."

"It's always made."

"Okay. Like I was saying, Molly, if there's anything—"

"I'm fine," she cut him off. "About the other day . . ."

"Forget it."

"If it's all the same, I'd rather not." She faced him from the kitchen doorway, the light behind her shining in her hair. "My timing's lousy, but I wouldn't take it back."

"I don't know what to say."

"Say 'Maybe.' It's a start, I figure."

He nodded. "Maybe."

"Did your friends connect?"

"What friends are those?"

She brought two steaming mugs and sat beside him on the sofa, close enough to make him nervous.

"Mutt and Jeff. They didn't leave their names. Somebody told them they could reach you here. They stopped by yesterday."

He felt the short hairs stirring on his nape. "What time?"

"Oh, noonish. I had Oprah on the tube. Something about the plight of lesbians in military service."

"Any message?"

"From the lesbians?"

"From Mutt and Jeff."

"Condolences for Glen," she said. "At first I thought they must be Metro, but they didn't say. It struck me funny that they would expect you to be here. I guess my reputation needs an overhaul."

"What else?"

"Jeff said they'll try and get in touch with you another time. And he was sorry that they missed you Friday night. Make sense?"

"It might."

"You want to fill me in?"

"I'd just be guessing. Do you keep a gun around the house?"

She frowned. "A .38. What is it, Jack?"

"It's loaded?"

"Useless, otherwise. You're scaring me."

"I don't think Mutt and Jeff expected me to be here, Molly."

"What, then?"

"They were sending me a message, telling me that they can reach the folks I care about."

Her hands were trembling as she set the coffee cup aside. "Why now?"

"I've got an angle on the men who murdered Glen—at least I *think* so. Friday night, a couple of torpedos tried to tag me out by Curtis Park."

" 'I'm sorry that we missed him.' " Molly repeated the words in a low voice as if she finally understood the joke.

"It wouldn't hurt for you to get away somewhere until I wrap this up."

"How long?"

He shrugged. "A week or two. It's hard to say."

"No sale." She shook her head. "I won't take Tommy on the road and live like fugitives. We'll just be careful."

"If you notice any strangers hanging out around the neighborhood—"

"I fire a warning shot between their eyes and punch up nine-one-one. No sweat."

"I don't like leaving you."

Her smile came back. "That's good to hear. Remember that when you get back in town."

"I will."

"You promise?"

"Absolutely."

Molly kissed him at the door. Not desperate, like the last time. Nice. A feeling he could easily get used to if he gave himself a chance and if Glen's ghost wasn't standing in the way.

"The gun," he said again when she had latched the screen.

"I won't forget. Take care."

He felt her watching as he crossed the lawn, retreating toward his rental car. Inside of him he nursed a deep, abiding hatred for Rodriguez and his goon squad, in or out of uniform.

He pictured Molly's visitors. No faces, but he knew their type. Broad shoulders, long on beef and attitude, with jackets covering their guns.

We'll be in touch.

He slid into the driver's seat and turned the engine over with an angry twist of the ignition key.

"Unless I touch you, first."

THE MIDDLE-CLASS apartment complex filled a block due east of Shenandoah Park. Somebody's Volvo hogged the numbered space assigned to Fowler, but he was easy, settling for an open piece of curb that put him closer to home. Instead of going for the beer first thing, he walked halfway around the complex to the rental office and the bank of mailboxes out front. Two bills and a religious tract comprised the daily catch.

Before he crossed the threshold of his apartment, Fowler knew that someone had come calling in his absence. Tacky after-shave and stale tobacco smoke were there to greet him, smells he did not recognize as belonging to any of his rare invited guests. The Glock was in his hand before he dropped his mail and closed the door behind him, double-locking it to slow the prowler down in case he was still inside.

A long shot, Fowler realized. The smell was fading, hours old. An open window would have carried it away in nothing flat.

But he would have to check it out regardless.

There was also a chance the unexpected caller might have left his card . . . or something else.

He scanned the smallish living room, found nothing out of place. The bathroom was likewise undisturbed, with the exception of a cigarette butt floating in the toilet bowl. The closet door was standing open in the bedroom, but his clothes were all in place, with no one hiding there or underneath the double bed.

If the prowler was not searching...then what? A show of force to keep him on his toes, just like the ploy of dropping by at Molly's on the pretext of a social call?

He found his answer in the kitchen when he opened the refrigerator to reach for a can of Coors. A hand grenade was braced against the partial six-pack, and Fowler stepped back a pace before he saw the safety ring and recognized it was a practice dummy, used to give recruits a feeling for the proper weight before they graduated to the real McCoy. He brought it out, the metal cold against his palm.

Propped behind the dummy pineapple was a Polaroid of Molly on her porch with broom in hand. He didn't need a dated negative to recognize the outfit she was wearing. Faded jeans and Metro T-shirt. Sandals on her feet.

Instinctively he turned the snapshot over and found a message printed there in square letters: Next Time.

His hand was on the telephone, one digit short of ringing her, before he caught himself. She knew the risk, and there was nothing to be gained by adding to her fears.

He cradled the receiver, picked it up again and tapped out Stano's number, waiting for the sound of a familiar voice.

"Hello?"

"It's Fowler."

"Shoot."

He spelled the problem out, extracting Rudy's promise that a covert team would be assigned to cover Molly Keegan and her son while he was out of town.

"It's really Metro's job, but what the hell."

"I owe you one," he said.

"Damn right. So wrap this fucker up and let's get on to something else, okay?"

Jack Fowler cracked a mirthless smile.

"We aim to please."

8

Ricky Kastor's favorite time of day was sundown, when the city came alive. It wasn't that Miami slept by daylight like an urban vampire, but the sun bleached out its buildings, streets and sidewalks. Everything was ordinary. Dull.

The night, by contrast, offered brilliant lights and dazzling colors, side by side with midnight shadows. Places where a man could hide himself away if there was any need. The night held secrets. Danger. Lust and pain.

The moment of transition, on the razor's edge of evening when the lights came on, was the time that Kastor cherished as his own. The rest of it was all downhill from there.

He had been weaned on darkness, with his mother working as a topless dancer and a cocktail waitress in assorted clubs, his old man hustling when and where he could, until he finally disappeared in Ricky's seventh year of life.

Good riddance.

Though school had been a minor inconvenience, Ricky stayed cool and picked up the knowledge he required to get along. Some math, the proper turn of phrase for all occasions. When he did his homework, it was mostly on the street, and he learned more by hanging out, listening and keeping his opinions to himself than any teacher in a classroom ever passed along.

The others taught him by example to know when a scam was ripe and when it could blow up. He learned to deal with heat—"Yes, sir" and "No, sir" when the uniforms were in his face, and how to judge which cops would walk away if they received a cut of the proceedings. He'd found out that violence was a tool like math and language, useful in specific situations and disastrous if it took control.

That was the major reason Ricky Kastor stayed away from drugs these days. A little grass around the house, of course—some blow at parties when the need arose—but dealing was another world, and Ricky had resigned himself to do without. Too many psychos on the street, all thinking they were Rambo Junior with their M-16s and KG-99s or whatever. Getting killed was bad for business, any way you tried to dress it up, and Ricky Kastor liked his life enough to try and hang around awhile.

On Monday evening Ricky watched the sunset through the bedroom windows of his sometime mistress, Lila Bush. It was her stage name. Ricky didn't know the name she was born with, and he didn't care. She worked as an exotic dancer—like his mom but softer, more at ease with herself—and that was all he had to know for now.

She listened, offered her opinion when he asked, and seemed to understand.

Of course, he did not tell her *everything*.

They had enjoyed the afternoon together, making love three times and competing with the brains on *Jeopardy* when they got tired. It tickled Ricky that he got the answers right so often, when he never went beyond eighth grade and there were guys from Mensa on the show who couldn't find their assholes if they used both hands.

Experience meant something after all.

Then it was sundown, and time for both of them to split for work. In Lila's case, that meant a club on Northwest Third, where she would dance three turns for thirteen bucks an hour plus the tips. She didn't trick with customers . . . or if she did, she was discreet, and Ricky would not have to know unless she brought a little something extra home some night. He figured she was smart enough to handle that herself, and if she blew it . . . well, it wouldn't be his first time with a needle in the ass.

Love hurts.

For Ricky, work meant stopping by the billiard hall an hour or so and checking the accounts or maybe staying for a game if he was in the mood. He missed the play these days, with other business crowding in, but that was how you got ahead in life. The rest of it, most any evening of the week, was hanging out at one of half a dozen favored clubs, observing what went down and tapping into rumbles from the street, collecting debts and putting wheels in motion for a brand-new round of deals.

He did not work the pigeon drop for chump change anymore, but Ricky liked a sting from time to time. Some bogus stocks and bonds perhaps, or something in real estate. The high-stakes floating crap game raided by "police" from central casting was a good one, but you couldn't pull it more than once or twice a year, if you were smart.

And Ricky was.

He knew exactly when to hustle, when to sting and when to walk away. In the twenty-odd years of caring for himself full-time, he had been forced to pull the trigger twice in self-defense. Word got around, and it was good enough as long as he avoided dealing pharmaceuticals where trigger-happy lunatics were calling the shots.

Providing the police with information was a sideline, risky on its face, but Ricky took precautions in his dealings with the law. It was the one phase of his business that he always handled solo, thereby cutting out the risk of witnesses and blackmail, or a pissed-off ex-employee looking for revenge. He dealt with certain trusted faces, knowing they were straight, prepared to walk the plank before they gave him up. He never passed on a bit of information unless at least one other person knew as much—or more—about the job at hand, and Ricky never, under any circumstances, ratted on an operation where he stood to clear a profit for himself.

When Lila finished in the shower, Ricky took his turn. They could have gone together, but he did not have the time or strength to play another round right then. They both had schedules to observe, and she was nearly dressed when Ricky left the bathroom, one towel wrapped around his head, another draped around his waist like a sarong.

"You look like Ghandi," Lila told him, grinning.

"He was skinnier than me."

"You have been putting on some pork."

"I've got your pork right here," he told her, whipping off the terry sarong.

"No time," she answered, stepping into heels that brought her up to Ricky's height. "I'm running late."

"You need to see the doctor?"

"Funny man." She kissed him lightly, cupped him with her hand and grinned as he involuntarily responded to her touch. "Still working, anyway."

"I'll show you work."

"Tomorrow, maybe. Gotta run."

He finished dressing in the semidarkness of her bedroom, watching as the lights came on outside. Miami was on fire with neon, every glowing sign a lure, extending promises that seldom were fulfilled. It was the only world where Ricky Kastor felt at home.

He heard the front door open then close again, and he smiled. "You miss me, Babe?"

"Don't push your luck."

The voice was gruff and male, belonging to the guy who occupied the bedroom doorway. He was six foot two or three and fairly solid, but he didn't need the muscle with that nickel-plated automatic in his hand. Behind him, number two was slightly shorter, with a thick mustache. His piece looked like a standard snub-nosed .38.

"You Ricky Kastor?"

"Who?"

"I thought so. Come along with us. We're going for a little ride."

"Says who?"

"Don't fuck around with Mr. Colt," the mustache said. "If we have to leave you here, we leave you dead."

"Well, since you put it that way..."

"See, I told you he was smart."

They let him lock the door, and surrounded him like bookends on the short walk to the elevator. No one in the lobby gave them a second, and they were on the street a moment later, moving toward a Buick Skylark parked against the curb in front, with a third man at the wheel. A red zone, by the hydrant, like they didn't give a damn.

Inside the car, the mustache brought a blindfold out and slipped it over Ricky's eyes. He took it as a hopeful sign.

If they were worried that he might remember where they took him, it suggested an intent to let him live...at least for now.

He clutched the slender straw and kept his mouth shut, wishing that he could remember how to pray.

"WE NEED some information," said Lieutenant Ervin Steele. "That's your department, so I'm told."

In front of him, the snitch named Ricky Kastor occupied a heavy wooden captain's chair, hands cuffed behind him, ankles bound with duct tape to the legs in front. The warehouse fronting Belle-Meade Drive was dark and cavernous around them, with a single bulb positioned over Kastor's head to cast a pool of light around the guest of honor. On the fringes of the light, Steele's men stood waiting, hungry predators who held themselves in check with difficulty, waiting for the word.

Kastor squinted in the glaring light and said, "I'm sorry, but you gentlemen are misinformed."

"You *will* be sorry if I have to ask a question twice," Steele promised him. He wasn't shouting like a maniac, the way some did when they were playing good-cop-bad-cop with a perp downtown. Experience had taught him that a quiet, reasoned tone conveyed more menace than a scream.

"If I could help you out, *believe* me, I'd be happy to oblige. The problem is—"

"The *problem* is," Steele interrupted, "that you've involved yourself in something that could eat you up alive. You fuck with me, I'll make you wish your mama had her tubes tied off, I swear to God."

The Stick was sweating, and not all of it from sitting underneath the light.

"Perhaps if I had some idea of what you wanted..."

"Fair enough. You like the races, Ricky?"

"Well..."

"The stock car races, maybe? Hialeah Speedway, for example?"

"I've been out that way from time to time."

"Last Friday night, I think it was. That ring a bell?"

"On Friday? Mmm...I do believe you're right."

"You had a friend there with you."

Kastor frowned, considering his options. "Most nights when I hit the track I go alone."

Steele snapped his fingers, and Skirvin moved in to stand in front of Kastor, reaching out to rip his shirt with one hand, while the other held a squarish plastic box against his thigh. Before the snitch could argue, Skirvin pressed the twin electrodes of the stun gun to his side and keyed the switch, a full two second's worth. The victim's body turned rigid, twisting, falling back.

"Okay, now." Steele gave Kastor time to catch his breath and sort out voices from the ringing in his ears. "The beauty of a stun gun is that it can't do lethal damage, see? I mean, if you were looking at a heart condition, maybe . . . but the way it is, no sweat. You want to be a tough guy, we can keep it up all night. Are we communicating, now?"

The snitch was staring back at Ervin Steele with fear and hatred in his eyes. A lethal mix, if their positions were reversed, but Steele held all the cards. He even had an extra stun gun waiting in case they ran the first one down before their pigeon cracked.

"I'll help you out," Steele said, accommodating to a fault. "We know your buddy's name already. Jackson Fowler, am I right?"

"I'm not a common snitch," said Kastor.

"No? I guess that means you charge a little extra for the shit your average junkie gives away. Is that about the size of it?"

"I don't have anything to say."

Steele nodded. Skirvin let him have another jolt, the perspiration acting as a perfect ground.

"Let's try again."

"Fuck . . . off."

Steele clipped the hustler with a backhand, opening his right cheek with a heavy signet ring.

"We've got a saying, Ricky: When you walked in here you had a pretty face and information, but you can't go home with both. I wouldn't say you're pretty, but the fact is you've got more to lose than looks if you keep jerking us around."

"I don't know what you want."

He sounded groggy. The lieutenant made a mental note to keep his temper, sparing any punches to the head that might defeat the purpose of their interview.

"Jack Fowler. Friday night. What did you talk about?"

"The races."

"Light him up."

Three seconds this time. Kastor thrashed like a marlin on a hook before he slumped back in his chair.

"I understand the need to prove yourself, believe me. You're a stand-up guy. The question you should ask yourself is: Would Fowler take this kind of heat for you?"

"What heat is that?"

"A sense of humor. Great. Once more."

The twin electrodes left red marks on either side of Kastor's nipple, like a snakebite that had somehow failed to break the skin.

"You know Jorge Rodriguez, Ricky? Nod your head if you have trouble answering."

"I heard the name." He sounded breathless, like a distance runner on the last leg of a marathon.

"You may not know it, but you're messing in his business now. That's not a healthy way to go."

"You think I'm moving coke?" He forced a smile. "That's bullshit. You can ask around."

"Nobody mentioned coke. That's not the issue. You've been telling tales."

"Says who?"

"Your buddy, Fowler. All I need from you is confirmation, certain details here and there."

"He's talking," Kastor said, "no reason he can't tell you everything you need to know."

"Again."

Kastor tried to flinch away from Skirvin and the stun gun, but there wasn't anyplace for him to go. His scream came out like someone moaning, with his voice box twisted in a knot.

"Wrong answer," Steele advised him. "When I say jump, you ask how high. I promise, it's the way to save yourself some pain." He gave the punk a moment to collect himself before saying, "Let's try again."

"We talked about his partner."

"So? I'm listening."

"His partner. Fowler's. Used to be. Got killed."

"That so?"

He nodded weakly, perspiration dripping off his chin to streak his chest. When he fell silent, Steele bent closer, prodding him.

"What else?"

"He wants the trigger. Payback."

"And he came to you?"

"Thought I might have a name."

"You didn't?"

Kastor shook his head, exhausted by the effort. "Told him maybe I could ask around."

"Well, there you go. Was that so bad?"

The snitch looked up at Steele with bleary eyes, as though he believed the worst was over. Play his cards right, and they could all be bosom pals and share a drink before he went back home.

"One thing," Steele said. "I want to make sure that I heard you right. Let's take it once more from the top."

They used another forty minutes and the stun gun's charge before he satisfied himself the snitch was holding nothing back. The Fed suspected dirty cops of taking Keegan down. Inquiries had been made, and Ricky had suggested Fowler find himself an independent dealer who was being squeezed. They had not been in touch again, and Kastor had no further progress to report.

Case closed, as far as Ricky was concerned.

"You've been a help," Steele said when Kastor took a break from wheezing. "One more little thing before we cut you loose."

"Whazzat?"

Steele grinned his brightest buddy-buddy smile. "You need to make a call."

9

The telephone caught Fowler in his jockey shorts, shower bound. His answering machine was on the job, but Fowler picked up when he recognized the voice.

"Hey, Jack? It's me. I've made some progress on that matter you were asking me about. When you get home—"

"I'm here."

"Oh, Jeez. I hate those fucking things."

There was a note of strain in Ricky Kastor's voice, but Fowler let it slide. "Me, too. What's happening?"

"I'm pretty sure I got those names you wanted."

"Wait a sec." He scrabbled for a pad and pencil on the nightstand and found them after several moments. "Okay, go ahead."

"Thing is, I need to *see* you," Kastor said. "These guys are heavy. I don't even like to talk about them on the phone."

"Goddamn it, Ricky..."

"If it's too much trouble, man, forget it. I just thought—"

"Where are you?"

"Jack, that isn't such a good idea."

"Don't yank me, Ricky. If you're looking for a meet, say where and when."

"You know a place called Billy Budd's, on Beacom?"

"I can find it."

"How's an hour sound to you?"

"I hope it's worth the trip."

"You won't be disappointed, man, I guarantee."

He looked up Billy Budd's in the directory. The bar was located near the point where Beacom met Southwest Seventh Street. To Fowler's knowledge, he had never seen the place. The neighborhood was average, but one never knew about a bar, and he did not feel like taking any chances.

For a start, the call from Ricky Kastor had been setting off alarms inside his head. It wasn't that he smelled a trap exactly, but the snitch's whole approach and attitude were... *different.* Fowler understood a certain paranoia when the telephone came into play, but meeting in the flesh was twice as dangerous. If Kastor did not mind alluding to their business on the phone, he might as well—

He shrugged it off. The meet was set, and Fowler was not backing out. But no one ever said he had to show up unprepared.

He skipped the shower, dressed quickly and slipped into his Jackass shoulder rig, then made sure the Glock was loaded to capacity before he stowed it underneath his arm. His backup weapon was a Colt 9-mm carbine, a domestic version of the classic Uzi submachine gun, fitted with a regulator to prevent full-auto fire. Removal of the regulator theoretically required an order from his boss, but Fowler didn't feel like calling Rudy Stano for advice. Instead he took a simple tool provided with the Colt and went to work.

Three minutes later, man and gun alike were set to rock and roll.

The folding stock let Fowler slip the automatic carbine and a pair of extra magazines inside an old gym bag. If things looked bad at Billy Budd's, the piece would fit beneath his jacket just as well.

He stood before the full-length mirror for a moment, bag in hand, to reassure himself the holstered Glock was not too obvious. When he was satisfied, he smiled and spoke to his reflection.

"Party time."

HE DID NOT NEED the hour, as it happened. Billy Budd's was less than half a mile from Fowler's home, but he allowed for traffic, driving north on Southwest Twenty-second Street and cutting west on Southwest Seventh, back to Beacom toward the bar.

In keeping with the nautical motif, a quarter-life-size galleon had been mounted on the roof, with lacquered sails that swelled before a nonexistent wind. He made a mental note to come around if they had any tropical storms that year so he could watch the midget galleon sail away for real.

He made a lazy circuit of the block, inspecting vehicles and passersby, alert for any overt symptoms of a trap. The joint was not exactly jumping, but he estimated some two dozen cars collected in the parking lot at Billy Budd's. Pedestrians were scattered here and there along the sidewalk, drifting in and out of other clubs. Most of them were paired by sex, and while that did not automatically preclude an ambush, it reduced the odds.

The second time around, he took it off the street and parked his rental in the spacious lot some distance from the other cars. He left the engine running for a moment, checking out the shadows, knowing he could overlook an army in the darkness, squinting in the glare of neon from the street. It took a moment just to pick out Ricky Kastor's pearl gray BMW, but there was no mistaking license plates that tagged him Mr. Pool.

There seemed to be a man behind the steering wheel, but Fowler could not swear he was alone, much less determine his identity. It stood to reason Kastor would be sitting in his own damned car, but you could never tell.

If things were always what they seemed, Miami would not rank consistently among the top-five murder zones in the Unites States.

"Okay."

Surprised to hear his own voice in the car, Jack bit his lip to stem the flow of words. Okay, he thought, he didn't come this far to sit and stare at Ricky's ride. It was time to get it done, or scrub the show and head on home.

He reached across the seat and slipped a hand in the gym bag, extracting extra carbine magazines and dropping one in each side pocket of his coat for balance. Next, the Colt itself, a live round in the chamber and the safety on as Fowler slipped it underneath his jacket, snug beneath his arm. A swivel harness would have helped, but he could reach it quick enough if anything went wrong.

At least he *hoped* he could.

The dome light illuminated Fowler as he left the car. He cursed and closed the door left-handed, cutting off the glare. He felt lopsided, awkward, with the carbine clasped beneath his arm like something from an old B movie where the monster walks around and drags one foot behind.

Just call me Igor, he told himself, grinning in the darkness as he stood beside the car, alive with nervous energy.

He made it to be forty feet at least to Kastor's vehicle from where he stood. Not far, a dozen strides or so, but it would seem like forty miles with someone shooting at him, open blacktop all the way. He thought about revising strategies and driving over, parking next to Ricky in that so-convenient empty space, but the empty space was almost *too* convenient. Prearranged, perhaps?

The automatic carbine pressed against his ribs as Fowler took the first step, followed by another. And the next. He felt like someone walking in a dream, his feet mired in gummy stickum from a giant Roach Motel and getting nowhere. Even so, he blinked and found that he had covered half the distance to the waiting BMW just like that.

No movement from the shadow-shape behind the wheel. He pictured Ricky sitting there and letting him do all the work, afraid to poke his head out where it might be taken for a target.

Fair enough.

If he had solid information on the men who killed Glen Keegan, Jack could easily forgive the snitch's eccentricity. If not . . .

He still had fifteen feet to travel when a Buick Regal nosed into the parking lot, its bright headlights tunneling the darkness. Fowler had a momentary glimpse of Ricky Kastor then, his head thrown back to show the shiny gash across his throat, and Fowler knew that he was dead. A sudden, furtive movement in the shadow of the BMW, and the trap was sprung.

The gunman should have had him cold, but he forgot to squeeze the trigger, jerking it instead, and Fowler heard the first shot snap past on his left. He sidestepped, crouching, swinging up the carbine as another round chipped asphalt at his feet.

He had no time for pinpoint marksmanship, and Fowler held the carbine's trigger down and ripped a burst across the BMW's grille, the headlight on the driver's side exploding, two or three rounds penetrating shadows where the gunman hid himself.

On Fowler's flank the Buick's brakes locked as the driver recognized that he was rolling toward a war zone. Someone screamed inside the car—a woman's voice— then a shotgun blast ripped through the driver's open window, fired at nearly point-blank range.

Jack swiveled toward his second adversary, running in a crouch and using Kastor's vehicle as temporary cover from the first man, knowing he would have to neutralize the scattergun to give himself a fighting chance. The second blast aimed in his direction more or less, but it was high. The pellets swarmed above his head, and Fowler used the muzzle-flash to guide his aim.

He caught the gunner with a rising burst that staggered him and dropped him to his knees. The guy had strength enough to work the shotgun's slide, but then he toppled over backward, squeezing off his last shot toward the stars.

The night dissolved into a string of fractured images for Fowler as he made his break: one shooter stretched out on the pavement, with at least one other still alive; the stalled Buick with its headlamps lighting up the battleground; a pistol shot that drilled the hem of Fowler's jacket when he turned to run.

He sprayed the shadows blindly, using up the last rounds in his magazine without a hope of scoring any hits, his adversary running like a quarterback with killer tackles on his heels and laying down a screen of cover fire.

Jack fumbled with a backup magazine and got it seated as another bullet stung his ankle, ricocheting off the pavement. Fowler answered with a burst that took the windows out of a Grand Prix and saw his target dodging, weaving, squeezing off his last two rounds.

Reloading on the run, the gunner ducked behind a Chevy van, and Fowler held his fire. Nobody else was shooting at him, and he had a hunch that there were only two assassins on the team. Advancing cautiously, he circled wide around the van to give himself a shot as soon as possible. His quarry would be moving, granted, but at least this way he had a chance.

The sudden glare of headlights blinded him, and Fowler knew at once he was not dealing with a regular patron from the club. Downrange the car left a standing start with smoking tires, its driver holding to a hard collision course. Jack aimed above the lights and fired off half a magazine in something like two seconds flat, without effect. A heartbeat prior to impact, Fowler threw himself aside.

Almost too late.

A numbing blow struck his left foot, spinning him around and dumping him on his side. He lost the carbine, heard it clatter on the pavement somewhere out of reach. The car was rocking to a stop, with a door flung open on the rider's side. A figure broke from the shadows, racing toward the car.

He sat up dizzily, groping for the pistol underneath his arm, and found it as the runner made his goal. The rider's door slammed shut as Fowler raised the Glock in a two-handed grip, and they were burning out of there before he fired. Two hasty rounds may have drilled the trunk or missed completely, and the car was rolling north on Beacom out of sight.

Pursuit was hopeless under the circumstances. Fowler struggled to his feet—his left leg throbbing with the dull, insistent pressure of a toothache—and he put the Glock away. After he retrieved his carbine from the pavement, he limped toward the gunner he had shot.

Correction, killed.

In life he would have stood around five-five, a stocky build and thick mustache, his dark hair styled. The dead man's clothes were stylish, and his 12-gauge was a 5-shot Ithaca. The sidearm worn beneath his jacket was a blue-steel Smith & Wesson Combat Magnum.

All of which spelled ''cop'' to Fowler, as he knelt beside the corpse. A gaggle of pedestrians had gathered several yards away, but no one raised a finger when he reached inside the dead man's bloodstained jacket, going through the pockets for a clue to his identity.

The wallet he retrieved contained a gold detective's badge and Metro-Dade ID card in the name of Stanley Hicks, age thirty-two. He dropped it in a pocket, fished his own badge out as sirens sounded in reaction to the shooting call.

The first ones on the scene would be patrolmen, and he did not want them going apeshit with a dead detective on their hands. That bit of news could wait for Rudy Stano and the federal shooting team.

He pulled the carbine's magazine and cleared the chamber, tuning out the gawkers as he settled back to wait.

"YOU'RE CLEAR with Metro-Dade so far," Rudy Stano said, tapping crusty ash from his cigar. "The chief was out for blood until we had a little chat. It's obvious the guy you capped blew up the two kids in the Regal, and we've got enough stray brass around the scene to prove that someone else was shooting, too. It's all 9 mm, but the firing pin and the extractor marks won't match your Colt. Throw in your buddy Kastor, and they've got some problems on their hands downtown."

"I'm glad to hear it."

"How's the foot?"

He flexed his toes and grimaced. "Sore."

"It serves you right. I ought to write you up for reckless action and endangering civilians."

"Chief—"

"You ever hear of backup on a deal like this? They've got this super new invention, Jack. It's called the telephone."

"I went to meet a snitch. It happens every day. You want to roll a SWAT team every time I get a phone call?"

"Bullshit, Jack. You were expecting trouble when you took the Colt along—without the regulator, I might add. You fucking *knew* it was a setup, and you froze me out."

"I *didn't* know. There was a chance, that's all."

"So now we've got three people dead—one of them a detective—and a nineteen-year-old girl in ICU. She's not expected to survive, but if she makes it through, she won't be fond of mirrors for a while. My phone's been ringing off the hook with newsies, and you know it has to be the same at Metro-Dade. Cop killed by Fed. They'll eat it up."

"Try 'dirty cop.' It fits."

"We're looking into that, but it takes time."

"His partner?"

"Has an alibi, of course. Seems he was catching up on paperwork last night. We have a confirmation from his boss."

"That wouldn't be..."

"Lieutenant Ervin Steele. You guessed it, Jack."

"Okay. I don't have any time to lose."

"Say what? You must be snorting confiscated merchandise if you think I'd let you go ahead with this shit coming down."

"I'll never have a better chance," said Fowler. "They're expecting me to sit it out while everybody and his cousin picks last night apart. As far as Steele knows, I'm immobilized."

"Damn right you are."

"But I don't *have* to be. A pit stop in the islands, Rudy. Two, three days should wrap it up with any luck."

"I'm not impressed with how your luck's been running lately."

"So I'm ready for a change."

"It stinks, Jack. You're already looking at a board on Hicks."

"Next week, that is. No way I'll miss it, if I catch a flight this afternoon."

"No way, unless Rodriguez and his playmates blow you up."

"In that case, you explain how I defied your standing orders, took off on my own to do a little hunting. If they drop me in a hole, you're free and clear."

"Fuck you. You think I operate that way?"

"I think we've got a one-time-only chance to nail Rodriguez and the bluesuits on his pad. It's worth the risk."

"You're pissed because they did your partner."

"Sure I am," said Fowler, "but that doesn't change the facts. The hit on Keegan is a handle, something we can use to bring these bastards down."

"You want to see down, Jack? Just look between your feet. Blow this one and there won't be any net to break your fall."

"It's cool."

"My ass. For all I know, you ought to be in traction with that leg. You gimp in here like Chester, and I'm supposed to put you in the field."

"I'll work it out. I'm fine."

"You're suicidal is what you are."

"It's all we've got."

Fowler had him there, but Stano was reluctant to concede defeat.

"What say we cover Steele and company with wires, surveillance, everything we've got? You put the shooting board behind you, and we jump back on Plan A."

"No good. They're not expecting me today. We've still got the advantage of surprise. A week from now it won't be worth the trip."

"You think they're bailing out?"

"Or covering their tracks. Whichever way it goes, we're on the clock."

"All right, goddamn it, take your shot. But if you fuck this up..."

"It's my ass on the line, remember?"

"*Both* our asses, Jack. The regional director won't be buying any lame excuses."

"I guess we'd better get it right the first time."

Stano frowned and took another drag on his cigar. "I guess that's right."

10

The flight to Nassau from Miami International took forty minutes, time enough for Fowler to enjoy a beer and contemplate the viper's nest that awaited him on the ground when he arrived. By all accounts, corruption had become a way of life in Nassau, surpassing anything Miami had to offer in its wildest dreams.

For starters, nature had apparently created Bahama as a perfect smuggler's paradise. Extending 760 miles along a northwest-southeast axis, seven hundred islands and at least two thousand islets—also known as cays—comprised the chain, with some three dozen of the larger islands presently inhabited by man. The rest were sand and coral, coves and virgin jungle, where any army of illicit traders could conduct their business undisturbed. Bimini, with its busy airstrip, was an hour from Miami Beach by speedboat, fifteen minutes in a private plane. When customs officers appeared, they mostly had their hands out and were not averse to loading cargo by themselves, if they were paid a little something extra for the job.

During prohibition, Bahama was a major source of foreign liquor bound for "Rum Row," off the eastern coast of the United States. A generation later, profits stemmed from new intoxicants, and by March 1979, the state police commissioner warned that the islands were being "deluged by drugs." But the ruling ministers in Nassau turned a deaf ear to his pleas for reinforcements, new equipment, better training for his men, preferring bland inaction while they waited endlessly for more "conclusive evidence."

So flagrant had the graft and money laundering become by 1983 that Lynden Pindling, the prime minister who had been installed by a syndicate of U.S. gamblers, was driven to establish an "independent" commission of inquiry to probe charges of government corruption and malfeasance. The commission sat for 146 days, interrogating some 360 witnesses and reviewing more than a thousand documents before its final report was issued . . . predictably exonerating the prime minister of any impropriety. Meanwhile the flow of drugs and cash continued, growing year by year, while Washington praised Pindling's "excellent cooperation" in the war against cocaine.

The cabin warning lights came on, and the pilot's disembodied voice announced their descent toward Nassau. Fowler cinched up his lap strap and delivered his empty beer can to the flight attendant on her final pass. Below him on the starboard side the green Caribbean was crystal clear and glassy calm.

They approached New Providence from the northwest, circling once over Nassau International Airport before executing a flawless landing. Fowler breezed through customs with his bogus travel documents made out in the name of Jason Fraser. In Miami, Rudy Stano had an operator standing by to handle any checkup calls to "Fraser's" listed business number and confirm that he was out of town for several days. A deeper check, with Metro-Dade or DEA, would show that Jason Fraser had been several times arrested on suspicion of importing drugs, but he had never come to trial. The scan would *not* reveal that Fraser had vanished into the federal witness protection program, abandoning his identity and launching a new life in the Pacific Northwest after furnishing information that led to indictments of several Florida dealers.

Fowler picked his luggage up and used a "Fraser" credit card to rent himself a car from Avis, tooling out of the airport and circling north of Lake Killarney, completing the seven-mile run to Nassau in just under ten minutes. It took him twice as long to navigate through downtown traffic, passing St. Bernard's Park and Government House, Rawson Square and Fort Fincastle, to reach his hotel on West Hill Street.

The Graycliff had been chosen with an eye toward style. A converted Georgian colonial house, it was the Caribbean's only five-star hotel, with rooms starting from $140 per day. In keeping with his cover as a prosperous coke dealer, Fowler had reserved himself a suite, its balcony overlooking the rose garden and flagstone veranda with its ornate central fountain.

A porter took his bags and led the way upstairs, departing with a smile and Fowler's tip. French doors were open on the balcony, a soft breeze ruffling the drapes. On it floated the scent of the garden just below...and something else.

Cheap after-shave.

The porter's? Fowler thought he would have noticed while the man was in the room. He shifted slightly, checking out the balcony itself, and glimpsed the profile of a stranger who was seated in a metal chair beyond the open doors.

In deference to Miami International's security, his pistol had been packed inside the smaller suitcase resting at his feet. He knelt and ran a thumb across the combination lock, and one hand was already inside the bag and searching when the stranger rose and turned to face him on the balcony.

"You won't need that," he said. "I'm Teddy Jakes."

"And you have paperwork to prove it, I suppose?"

"Sure thing."

Fowler left the open bag and crossed the room to meet his uninvited visitor halfway. The federal badge and ID card seemed genuine enough, and Fowler let himself relax a fraction as he passed them back.

His Nassau contact was a trim, athletic-looking man of six foot one or two, fair-haired and freckled from the year-round sunshine. His complexion was the sort that stubbornly resisted a tan despite the climate, making him look vaguely out of place. For all that, Rudy Stano had described him as a competent and energetic agent in the field.

"Good flight?"

"It got me here."

"I took the liberty of checking out your suite. It's clean, so far."

"That won't mean squat if someone made you coming in."

"It's not a problem. I've got friends on staff."

"I hope you're right."

"Relax. This afternoon may be your only chance."

"You won't mind talking while I put some things away?"

His contact shrugged and found himself a chair. "No sweat."

The first thing Jack extracted from his luggage was the shoulder holster, with his Glock and extra magazines. He shed his lightweight jacket, slipped the holster on and covered it again.

"You came prepared."

"It's been that kind of week."

"I wouldn't count on any heavy action here in Nassau, but you never know. You're trolling for a major fish, I understand."

"Jorge Rodriguez and a couple of his friends."

"He's got a place across the harbor, out on Paradise, but no one's home."

"I'll find him when I'm ready," Fowler said. "Right now I'm working on the paper trail."

"In that case, you can say 'Eureka,' friend, because you've found the mother lode."

"That solid?"

"Better. The Rodriguez family has been working out of Bahama for six or seven years. They started running flake and paying for protection by the load, until Jorge found out how easy life could be away from Medellín. These days he greases everybody worth the effort and divides his time between Miami and the house on Paradise. Colombia won't see him more than two, three times a year, on weekend visits."

"He's been moving up."

"You bet. The ISD—that's state police, the Internal Security Division—knows every move he makes in Bahama, but they're not allowed to touch him. Too much juice upstairs."

Jack finished hanging up his suits and started folding dress shirts into scented drawers. He said, "We ought to have a decent shot at intercepting shipments, even so."

"You'd think so," Jakes replied. "One problem is, his people broadcast over VHF, the aviation band. Try scanning 720 different channels when they hold transmissions down to four, five seconds, max. Sometimes we spot them going out, but tracking them gets pretty rough."

"No help from the Bahamian authorities?"

"Oh, sure. They aren't *all* bought and paid for, necessarily. I know some boys at ISD, some others on the Nassau force, who hate the way things stand. The flip side is that for every honest cop you've got another one who's on the pad or doesn't like the foreign competition on his own home turf."

"Some kind of jurisdictional dispute?"

Jakes wore a strained, ironic smile. "A case in point," he said. "A few years back, on Independence Day, when everyone was celebrating in the streets, a cartel pilot started making passes over Clifford Park and dropping leaflets. 'DEA Go Home.' Each leaflet had a hundred-dollar bill attached to make the point. Later I found out they were run off by a printer who does business with the government—specifically, the ISD."

"You're telling me it's not a milk run. I already knew that going in."

"It's more than that. I've lost three snitches in the past six months. One of them turned up in the harbor, what the sharks spit out. The other two are carried on the books as missing, with presumption of foul play."

"Rodriguez."

"It's his style, but I'd be stretching if I told you he approved the contracts. He's got standing orders to eliminate informants, infiltrators, anyone who rocks the boat. A thousand-dollar bounty, payable to anyone who makes the tag, if he can show the mark was working to subvert Rodriguez."

"And if they can't?"

Jakes shrugged. "The mark's still dead, and Jorge saves himself a grand. I couldn't prove it to a judge, but I've been told there are some snakes at ISD who grab those bounties every chance they get."

"I wouldn't be surprised. Miami's finest have been known to turn a trick or two."

"I heard. That is, they briefed me on your partner."

"Oh?"

"It's need-to-know, don't worry. As it is, I've got a stake in how your play goes down."

"Agreed. We'll need to minimize our public contact, even so."

"It's taken care of. I'll be hanging out around the office if you need me, but your lifeguard is a local, Weldon Glass."

"A snitch?"

"Deep-cover ISD." Jakes saw the frown on Fowler's face and raised an open hand. "Don't worry, this one's clean. He also hates Rodriguez, ever since the family iced a couple of his buddies some time back. For what its worth in Nassau, Weldon holds a grudge."

"You'd stake your life on that?"

"I have. He won't do anything to rat you out, and his immediate superiors are in the dark about your mission. If they find out you've been seen together, they'll assume you're just another stateside dealer he's been checking out."

It ran against the grain for him to trust in strangers, but he seemed to have no choice. Reluctantly Jack Fowler nodded, settling in an easy chair across from Jakes.

"Okay, I'll try him on for size. Who else is in the picture as of now?"

"Unless you stumble over a familiar face, there's only the regional director," Jakes replied. "We're tight as we can be."

"I'll watch my step," Fowler said. "You want to fill me in on the Rodriguez operation locally?"

"It's pretty standard, for a staging area. The shit comes in direct from La Guaira if they're feeling cocky, sometimes out of Port-au-Prince or Kingston if they feel like greasing middlemen. From here you've got a straight shot to Miami or the Keys from Bimini, Abaco, Grand Bahama, Andros—name your port of preference. I wouldn't want to guess how many flights take off from Bahama in a given week, much less the yachts and speedboats dropping over for a day or two. The ISD could never stop them all, even if they were playing straight. They way it is, they pick off less than one percent.''

"So much for 'excellent cooperation,'" Fowler said.

Jakes smiled. "You know the way things work in Washington. If the director started pointing fingers, we'd be out of here so fast they'd have to send our footprints on a different flight. As is, we smile in public and do everything we can to square accounts behind the scenes. At least it isn't open season on our people, like in Colombia and Mexico."

"I need to get a grip on the financial end of things. Someplace Rodriguez banks, if I can pull it off."

"Ask Weldon when you see him. He can quote the scripture on Jorge from memory, chapter and verse. If there's a way inside, he'll know it."

"When are we connecting?"

"How about tonight?"

"Suits me."

Jakes did not have to mention that a man in his position walked a tightrope, mixing arrogance and urgency. The timing of a shipment might be critical, but local dealers would respond to any hint of desperation much the way sharks react to blood in the water, turning savagely upon their chosen prey. Successful smugglers had to keep their cool and deal from strength—and agents working under cover had to do the same to keep themselves alive.

"I took the liberty of booking you a reservation at the Pilot House," Jakes said. "Best seafood on the island, and they're not particular about their clientele."

"Terrific."

"No offense," Jakes said, "but it's a place where dealers go to let their hair down, make a few connections when they're new in Nassau. The Rodriguez people see you sitting down with Weldon there, and they won't think twice.''

"You hope."

"It's cool. You won't get hassled while you're talking shop, and you can lay the groundwork for a contact with the family, Weldon serving as your go-between. They know him well enough to take the bait.''

"We pull this off, it stands to leave your local boy exposed.''

"Take Rodriguez down, and it won't make any difference. If you blow it . . . well, let's think about that, if and when.''

"Who runs the local action for Rodriguez?''

"He's got a cousin on the island, Rafael Ornelas, but the deals get made by Gorman Poole. He's like the unofficial minister of dope for Bahama under Pindling's wing. The guy's been in and out of government a dozen times since independence, but he's always been connected where it counts. These days they've got him on the payroll as an 'economic analyst' in Freeport, watching over the casinos and collecting payoffs from the Grand Bahama Port Authority. It leaves him ample time to run his import-export business on the side.''

"So he's the pipeline?''

"One of them, at least. Connect with Poole and you're halfway home.''

"I'm looking forward to it.''

"Eight o'clock," said Jakes. "You're driving?''

"Yes.''

"You'll find the place on Village Road. Can't miss it, really. Weldon will be looking for you in the bar, from half-past seven on.''

It troubled Fowler, having to rely on strangers from the start, but he appeared to have no choice.

"All right."

"I'd better hit the bricks. You have my number if you need me."

Fowler let him out and double-locked the door behind him, poured himself a double whiskey from the minibar and took it to the balcony. The hotel parking area was out of sight, behind some palms on Fowler's left, but he imagined Teddy Jakes retreating toward a standard-issue compact car.

One hour on the island, and his cover had been jeopardized by contact in his suite. Jakes obviously trusted his connections on the hotel staff, but Fowler did not have that luxury. From this point on, a single glitch would be enough to get him killed.

He sipped his whiskey, staring off across the gardens into space, his mind preoccupied with brooding thoughts. Another meeting still ahead, with one more stranger who could get him killed. It was the only game in town, but Fowler had already seen enough to know he did not like the rules.

With any luck, he thought, there just might be a way to shift the odds.

And make it through the night alive.

11

He turned the shower on as hot as he could stand and faced the needle spray, intent on steaming every trace of weariness and anger from his pores. Despite the first-class pampering, his flight had left Jack Fowler feeling vaguely rumpled, like his suit. He needed to be fresh and keep his wits about him when he faced the enemy.

When he was lobster red and tingling from his scalp down to his feet, he switched the temperature control to cold to let the shock revive him, shivering as the goose-flesh rippled on his back and arms. The sudden chill helped dampen Fowler's rage, a fire within him that had burned nonstop since Rudy Stano broke the news of Keegan's death. The two attempts on Fowler's life, together with the threat against Glen's family, combined to feed that inner flame, but he could not afford the luxury of rage tonight.

He needed *cool,* if he was going to survive.

Successful agents, in his own experience, possessed the very qualities that kept a low-life like Jorge Rodriguez going strong: a measure of detachment from the violence in their daily lives; a certain distance, carefully maintained, between their hearts and minds. The moment that an agent—or a dealer—started thinking like a normal human being, he was riding for a fall.

The world they shared as adversaries was a place of shadows, black and white mixed to murky shades of gray. The rules were hard enough to understand if you were focused on a certain goal; without that focus, careless players were as good as dead.

He turned the shower off and stepped out on the bath mat, dripping. The terry towel was rough against his skin, and Fowler used it vigorously, bringing circulation back to arms and legs. When he was done, he draped the towel across the shower rod and padded naked from the bathroom, picking out a lightweight suit to match the balmy evening temperature.

Still barefoot, sitting on the bed in shirt and slacks, he stripped the Glock and reassembled it with practiced motions, barely glancing at his busy hands. Before reloading, Fowler worked the slide and dry-fired several times to test the mechanism, finally satisfied as he replaced the magazine and jacked a round into the chamber.

Dressed to kill, he chose a pair of slip-on loafers, covered up the shoulder holster with his jacket, then made his way downstairs. He still had time to kill before his date with Weldon Glass, and Fowler spent it in the hotel bar, nursing a whiskey and watching the tourists filter in. The Graycliff's clientele ran toward professionals, a few with spouses, more with younger "traveling companions." They were money on the hoof, with Rolex watches, Gucci bags and footwear, custom-tailored clothing and coiffures. They spoke in cultivated accents ranging from the Bourbon South to Martha's Vineyard, but it all came out the same: discussing money, where it came from, where it went.

Observing them, he thought the real-life Jason Fraser would have felt at home among the brokers, surgeons and attorneys mingling at the bar. At one time or another, he or someone like him had undoubtedly supplied these very pillars of society with crystal fuel for private fantasies.

He tired of watching them at last and finished off his whiskey, left five dollars with his empty glass and strolled out to the parking lot. From force of habit, Fowler checked around the rental car for signs of tampering, but he stopped short of opening the hood or crawling underneath to look for hidden bombs.

If someone wanted him in Nassau, they would find him. There was no point dwelling on the risk, but he would watch his back as always and protect himself where possible.

Emerging from the hotel parking lot, he found he had an hour left to kill. Five years had passed since Fowler visited the island last, and he refreshed his memory by circling the downtown sprawl, past Windsor Park and north on East Street, back along the harbor front with Paradise Island a quarter mile to his left. He could not see the home away from home Jorge Rodriguez had constructed for himself, but Fowler sensed his presence like a stain on the landscape.

He reached the Pilot House with twenty minutes left to spare and tipped a young valet to park his car. Inside, a hostess in a slinky formal steered him toward the bar, reminding him politely that his reservation had been booked for eight o'clock, not seven forty-five. He took the hint and ordered one more whiskey, sipping as he scanned the room's dark paneling and nautical accoutrements. Harpoons and life preservers were interspersed with navigational devices on the walls, and a weathered mermaid figurehead dominated the space behind the bar.

The clientele included two male blacks and half a dozen tourist couples, each maintaining distance from the others as they huddled over their expensive drinks. He was about to guess which of the blacks would be his contact, when another suddenly appeared and settled on the empty stool beside him.

"Jason Fraser?"

"Right."

The undercover narc stuck out a hand and forced a smile that did not seem to fit his mood.

"I'm Weldon Glass."

THE WORST PART of his job, thought Weldon Glass, was the requirement that he meet periodically with total strangers and either set them up for an arrest or try to help them out with problems of their own if they were members of "cooperating agencies." He had become accustomed to the local pushers, Yankee smugglers and the front men for Colombian cartels, but every new face was a wild card, a potential killer if he dropped his guard a fraction of an inch.

All things considered, Glass felt better dealing with a strange narcotics dealer than an unknown cop. With dealers, you already knew where they were coming from—a ruthless profit motive, buttressed by sadistic violence when the need arose. Strange cops, by contrast, might be anything from vengeance-bent crusaders to corrupted servants of the very criminals they swore to put in jail.

Eleven years of trying to enforce the law in Nassau had persuaded Glass that most men had a price, and those who didn't, frequently approached their mission from a viewpoint that was neither realistic nor entirely sane. The straight professionals, in his experience, were few and far between. No matter how you tried to walk around the problem, working in the field with crooked cops or crazy cops could get you killed.

The grudging partnership with Teddy Jakes and the DEA in Nassau had been forced on Weldon Glass by his superiors, a symbol of the "excellent cooperation" touted by some fuzzy-headed journalists in Washington. Glass knew that he was not, in fact, expected to cooperate beyond the minimal requirements of reluctant allies going through the motions, and he had devoted several weeks to scrutinizing Jakes, investigating his performance and connections in the same way a potential enemy was studied. In time he came to understand that Teddy Jakes was an honest cop who was committed to the Herculean task of shutting down Colombia's Bahamian connection with the States.

Their partnership, so far, had failed to set the world on fire. For prosecution in the islands to proceed, Glass had to pass his information on to various superiors—themselves too often bought and paid for by the subjects of his latest probe. The Pindling government was riddled with corruption from its leader to the lowly rank and file, a system that rewarded avarice and punished virtue while maintaining the facade of an enlightened modern state. Increasingly Glass found himself supplying information to the DEA through Teddy Jakes, while holding back from his superiors at ISD.

It should have been enough that Jakes endorsed his latest contact, but they lived in times when Vice detectives in Miami went to jail for murder, and an agent of the hallowed FBI was serving time for selling secrets to the KGB. In a disordered world, endorsements simply weren't enough. Glass had to judge a stranger for himself before he put his life in unfamiliar hands.

He waited for his contact in the self-serve parking lot, ignoring the valets and being carefully ignored in turn. Black patrons of the Pilot House were mostly businessmen or functionaries of the state, with drivers paid to wait outside while they were entertained. As Glass arrived on wheels, and posed no threat to the valets or vehicles left in their care, he was dismissed without a second thought.

Effectively invisible, he watched the agent known as Fraser—certain to be an alias—drop off his rented car and step inside the restaurant. Glass waited several moments before he followed, giving Fraser ample time to find the bar and settle in, then strolled through the heavy oaken doors. The hostess let him find his own way to the bar, and Glass hung back to study Fraser for a moment, prior to moving in.

The man seemed perfectly at ease, no first-time jitters, and his jacket had been cut to more or less disguise the fact that he was armed. Glass knew the basic outline of his cover—a Miami dealer, looking for a source in the Rodriguez family—and the Bahamian assumed that he was earmarked as the go-between. Before he fell in step, however, he would have to judge the stranger's mettle for himself. If Fraser passed inspection, Glass would see what he could do. If not...well, Teddy Jakes had learned to live with disappointment in the past.

There were two black men in the bar, and Glass saw Fraser surreptitiously examine both of them, as though expecting something in the nature of a sign from the man he was supposed to meet. When one of them got up to leave, Glass used the opportunity to close on Fraser's blind side, settling on the vacant stool as if it was reserved. He gave the American points for not reacting with surprise at his appearance.

"Jason Fraser?"

"Right."

"I'm Weldon Glass."

The handshake was firm and dry, without the sort of knuckle crunching some Americans regarded as obligatory.

"Are you drinking?"

"Rum and coke."

His contact ordered, paid the tab, turned down a refill on his whiskey. "So, you made me coming in?"

"Our mutual acquaintance gave me your description."

Fraser frowned at that, a cautious man reacting to the news that someone is discussing him behind his back, but it was clearly unavoidable. "You know my business, too, I guess."

He was about to answer when the hostess interrupted them, informing Fraser that his table was available. She registered a moment of surprise at finding them together, and Glass responded with a look that put her in her place before he rose and trailed his contact toward the dining room.

They shared a private booth, remote enough from other tables that they would not have to whisper when they spoke. Glass ordered lobster, with a seafood salad on the side, and Fowler followed suit. When they were left alone, he faced the black man squarely, getting down to business.

"I've been told you can put me next to Gorman Poole."

"It's possible," Glass said, "if you've got cash to spend."

"A hundred thousand confiscated dollars ought to break the ice."

Glass frowned. "He'll take your money, right enough, but you'd be dreaming if you think the ISD will ever drop a net on Poole."

"It isn't Poole I want."

"Ornelas?"

"Now you're getting warm."

"He doesn't meet just anybody, Mr. Fraser. Someone should have told you that."

"I got the word. My hunch is, he can spare some time for someone offering a million bucks a month."

"He might, at that."

"So, can you get me an appointment with his front or not?"

"I can, but it may take some time."

"The hundred thousand is for Poole, if he can clear a slot tomorrow or the next day, max. I don't have time to dick around."

"He won't take kindly to an ultimatum."

"Use your charm, but get the point across. My time is money, just like his."

"I'll see what I can do. No promises."

"There's something else."

"Which is?"

"Rodriguez and his playmates launder sixty-one percent of their illicit cash through Merchants Bank of Nassau. What I need from you is someone I can touch, inside, to document the family link with various accounts."

Glass frowned. "Our laws concerning the disclosure of financial information and identities on numbered bank accounts are very strict. A member of the staff would risk his liberty if he agreed to testify, and you would never make a local prosecution stick in any case."

"I wasn't thinking local," Fowler said. "If I can prove a drug connection on the flow of cash from Merchants Bank to the Unites States, we're authorized by federal law to seize the cartel's assets, bank accounts included. On the side, I have a sneaking hunch the IRS would like to make a case against Rodriguez for exporting untaxed cash."

"It still requires a member of the staff at Merchants Bank to sacrifice himself."

"Not necessarily. With banking documents in hand, we demonstrate a link between accounts in Nassau and Miami, and a federal judge okays the asset seizure. If

Rodriguez wants his money back, he has to plead his case in court.''

"The documents you seek would be illegally obtained," said Glass. "Is that a problem?"

Fowler shook his head. "My reading is, our search and seizure rules apply on U.S. soil. If someone at the bank hands over voluntary evidence, we're free and clear. The only rub would be potential prosecution here in Nassau, and the DEA won't name a source at any price. We get that far, I can foresee some bank officials copping pleas around Miami, coming up with all the documented evidence we need."

The waiter brought their food, and both men spent the next few moments savoring the rich broiled lobster, melted butter, and the best house wine. The thought of Rudy Stano cursing when he saw the voucher for the meal made Jack enjoy it all the more.

"I know a person who might help," Glass said at last, "but there are risks involved."

"I'm well aware of that."

Ignoring him, the man from ISD went on. "The banking laws are one thing, but Rodriguez and Ornelas do not prosecute their enemies in court. The person who assists you must be conscious of the dangers and accept them voluntarily."

"So far, so good."

"I may agree to pass your name along, but first I have a question you must answer honestly."

"I'm listening."

"Why is it that you wish to break Rodriguez?"

"It's my job."

Glass shook his head. "Not good enough. I want the truth."

"All right. I used to work Narcotics out of Metro-Dade, Miami, and my partner stayed behind when I went federal. We were friends for close to fifteen years. Last month Rodriguez had him killed. The trigger may have been a dirty cop. I want them both.''

Glass stared at Fowler for a moment, never breaking contact with his eyes. It felt as though he were peering into Fowler's brain and sifting through his words in search of lies.

At length the black man said, ''I'll make some calls tonight. The meet with Poole should not be difficult. As for the rest, I make no promises.''

That said, Glass turned his full attention back to the crustacean on his plate. He was not giving anything away, but Fowler liked his style. It helped to know that when the chips were down, your contact in a shaky system valued loyalty over job description. He trusted Weldon Glass so far, but caution ran both ways. He was prepared to break the link at any time if he had reason to believe the man from ISD was stringing him along.

First up, a face-to-face with Gorman Poole to pave the way for a potential meet with Rafael Ornelas. If Glass's contact at the Merchants Bank came through, so much the better. And if not . . .

Then he would find another way to get the information he required. Make contacts of his own and *buy* the paperwork, if it came down to that.

The evidence existed; Fowler was convinced of that. A banking system proud of its security was never short on paperwork to document transactions, and the holders of accounts would have to be identified—on microfilm, computer disk, whatever.

It was Fowler's job to find his way inside the maze, retrieve the crucial names and come back out again.

The trick was coming out of it alive.

12

The call from Weldon Glass came through an hour short of dawn. The travel clock on Fowler's nightstand told him it was 6:05 a.m., and the remnants of a troubled dream were still clinging in his mind like cobwebs as he fumbled for the telephone.

"Hello?"

"You want to meet with Poole, be in front of your hotel at nine o'clock. We have to see the man in Freeport if you want to play."

"Nine sharp."

"Be punctual."

The line went dead, and Fowler cradled the receiver, rolling over on his back. The dream was gone, its details lost, a residue of vague uneasiness its only legacy. He closed his eyes and saw Glen Keegan's face, then Molly's. Finally Jorge Rodriguez, grinning like a hungry shark.

Sleep squirmed away from him, retreating out of reach. He sat up in the king-size bed and stretched to reach the lamp, expelling darkness to the corners of the room where it could crouch and hide. It was too early for a breakfast call, but Fowler's restlessness took over and he hit the shower, shaved, and dressed with more than usual attention to his clothes.

For Gorman Poole and Freeport, it would pay to look just right.

Located on Grand Bahama, fifty miles west of Florida's Gold Coast, Freeport was the entertainment capital of Bahama. It was also a throwback to white colonial rule in the islands, a virtual state within a state, dominated by descendants of the racist "Bay Street Boys" in their new incarnation as the Grand Bahama Port Authority. The brainchild of stock manipulator Wallace Groves and his sidekick, Sir Stafford Sands, the Port Authority ostensibly existed to maintain a deep-water port for the benefit of heavy industry in Bahama. In fact, the group was bankrolled by shady deals on Wall Street and covert donations from the Lansky-Dalitz syndicate in Florida, Las Vegas and New York. The mobsters had their eyes on new casino licenses—locally dubbed "certificates of exemption"—which they obtained without delay once Lynden Pindling took his station at the helm of government in 1967. Other establishments followed on Paradise Island, linked to Nassau by a two-million-dollar toll bridge, but Freeport remained preeminent, the Port Authority conducting business as a law unto itself. In cases where a strong executive might otherwise have intervened, six-figure "loans" and contributions for "election expenses" insured Pindling's silence and continued cooperation with the Port Authority.

It was an atmosphere where members of the drug cartel could prosper, at a price. Protection was not cheap, but the beneficiary of earnings in the neighborhood of three billion tax-free dollars yearly could afford to spread a little of the wealth around.

From what he knew of Freeport, Fowler understood that the casinos were controlled—at least behind the scenes—by second-and third-generation Meyer Lansky types, adept at skimming profits and manipulating books, returning dirty cash to the Unites States as loans with spotless pedigrees. They weren't averse to violence in defense of profit margins, but they kept it to a minimum and tried to be discreet.

The drug cartels were something else entirely. Weaned on human blood in Medellín and Cali, hardened by *La Violencia* until the murder and dismemberment of human beings meant no more than stepping on an ant, the cocaine cowboys made their gambling neighbors nervous. There had been no open clash so far, and cash had covered ruffled feelings, but the day was coming—Fowler knew it in his heart—when north and south would come to blows.

He wondered idly if the old-line Mafia still had the guts to go the distance with the new breed from Colombia, relentless businessmen who already dominated eighty percent of cocaine distribution in America. The Sicilians had been largely ousted from the narco trade by blacks, Latinos, Orientals, Arabs, Corsicans...and something had to give.

Jack Fowler only hoped it would not give today—not here, not now.

He ordered breakfast up from room service at seven-thirty—scrambled eggs and crispy bacon, half a grapefruit, coffee, toast and marmalade. He ate it all, went back to brush his teeth a second time, retrieve his leather bag of earnest money from the Graycliff's vault and still had time to reach the street outside with forty seconds left to spare.

A baby-blue Mercedes pulled up on the stroke of nine o'clock, the tinted driver's window gliding down to show the solemn face of Weldon Glass behind the wheel.

"All ready, mon?"

"As ready as I'll be."

"We best be going, then. These people don't like waiting, if you follow."

Fowler placed the leather satchel on the floor between his feet and kept his jacket open so that he could reach the Glock a little easier if they were stopped along the way. With Glass in charge of navigation, he made no attempt to see if they were followed from the Graycliff to the airport, seven miles due west of Nassau.

He was mellow, with his mind made up to deal with problems if and when they reared their heads. Until he could identify and isolate the enemy, he was a dealer on vacation, killing time and looking for a score.

The future was an empty slate that he could write upon with chalk or blood, depending on his mood and the approach his adversaries used.

Right now, Jack Fowler felt that he could play it either way.

THE FLIGHT from Nassau International to Freeport's modern airport used up twenty minutes of their time. They stepped out into sunshine and the smell of steaming asphalt, sounds of traffic, and a view of the Lucayan Beach Hotel-Casino taking up a fair chunk of the Freeport skyline to the south. A car was waiting for them, and they both got in the back, the silent driver and another bruiser riding shotgun up in front.

They parked in front of the Lucayan Beach and caught a treadmill to the entryway—the self-same "moving sidewalk" pioneered around Las Vegas more than thirty years ago. The tall glass doors were automatic, opening to greet them with a gust of frosty air that prompted Fowler to ad lib a prayer of thanks for air-conditioning.

In terms of architecture and logistics, the Lucayan Beach was nothing Fowler had not seen a hundred times in Vegas or Atlantic City. There were superficial differences, of course—the tropical motif, the Calypso rhythms—but the strategic layout was the same as any other fancy clip joint in the world. Upon arrival the visitor was instantly confronted with the grand casino—slot machines up front for impulse players, with the green-felt gaming tables spreading out behind. The hotel registration desk, the rest rooms, the elevators, shops or restaurants could not be reached without a mandatory stroll past banks of slots, the tables sporting dice and blackjack, poker and roulette, chemin de fer and baccarat. There was a busy sports book tucked away on Fowler's right where guests could lay their bets on any race, athletic contest or election in the Western Hemisphere.

"Too bad you can't afford to bet what's in the bag," said Weldon Glass.

"You kidding me? The only kind of luck I've ever had with gambling is bad."

"But still, the risk..."

"It's only risky if you think you've got a chance to win. Beyond that, you're just tossing money in the fire. Where's Poole?"

"He has a suite upstairs."

"I had a feeling that he might."

From what he knew of Gorman Poole, it seemed to Fowler that their contact was the Nassau government's official man-on-site in Freeport. He collected payoffs, supervised casino counts to guarantee the proper "tax" was paid, and pulled assorted strings to minimize embarrassment when things got out of hand. A scuffle at the gaming tables, or a body in the surf, and Poole could smooth things over...for a price. It was reported and confirmed from independent sources that he also took a bite from any contraband that passed through Bahama on its way to somewhere else, the shifting tariff rate depending on Poole's mood, the quantity of product being moved and the attendant risks involved.

In short he was a fixer, and he seemed to know his job.

With Glass in the lead, they proceeded through the heart of the casino. Business was light that early in the morning. Roughly half the card tables were unattended, the remainder manned by dealers facing one or two hung over players apiece. The roulette wheel spun and rattled for an audience of three, and there was no one shooting craps at all.

"Slow morning?"

His companion shrugged. "The tourists are like insects. They come out at night to feed themselves and flit around the lights."

"I hear some bitterness in there."

"My country lives on tourist dollars, plus the drugs and banking from America. I understand priorities," Glass said, "but I am not obliged to venerate the pigs involved."

They reached the elevators, waited for the door to open, stepped inside. Glass punched a button, and they were on their way to the fifth floor. No penthouse for the likes of Gorman Poole when he could keep his action closer to the playing floor and still avoid those prying eyes.

Two heavies met them in the corridor outside Poole's suite. The frisk was brief, professional, removing Fowler's sidearm; Glass was clean. The bruisers did not bat an eye as they poked through the bundled cash in Fowler's satchel, finally satisfied there were no weapons or explosives underneath.

One of the spotters faded back and knocked on Gorman's door. A striking redhead in a formfitting jumpsuit answered. She listened, nodded, then beckoned for Glass and Fowler to proceed. They left the heavies on the doorstep, standing watch.

"This way, please."

From her voice, Jack thought she might have been a singer. Rich and sultry, it seemed made for smoky ballads where a lady takes the blues and turns it into something sensual, instead of merely sad. They followed her beyond the foyer, through a sitting room with closed doors on either side. Their destination was a shaded balcony where Gorman Poole sat waiting in a flowered shirt and starched white shorts, presiding at a wrought iron table painted white to match its empty chairs.

Jack recognized the man from photos in the files at the DEA Miami—short and stout, his close-cropped hair and drooping mustache flecked with gray, much like the ash on his cigar. The rings that covered both hands like designer knuckle-dusters would be solid gold, each bright with precious stones.

Poole rose to greet them, shaking hands with Weldon first and letting him complete the introductions, ordering a round of whiskeys from the redhead as she turned away. She didn't seem to hear him, but the drinks—all doubles—were in front of them a moment later, tinkling with ice.

"I'm pleased to meet you, Mr. Fraser, but you know the saying Time is Money?"

"I'm familiar with the sentiment," Jack answered, handing Poole the satchel full of confiscated hundred-dollar bills. "A simple token of appreciation...for your time and courtesy."

"A man of etiquette. That pleases me."

Poole took the bag and placed it on the deck beside his chair. He did not open it or try to count the cash inside. Glass would have given him a figure on the telephone, and any shortage would be treated as an insult, grave enough to queer whatever deals they made today.

"What is it that you wish to ask, my friend?"

Jack cleared his throat. "I represent a group of men in the United States who deal in recreational supplies. Jamaica and Colombia provides the merchandise, but there are sometimes transportation difficulties, if you follow me."

"Of course."

"We need a more reliable supplier, one whose lines of transportation are secure. I'm told that you may know of such a man."

"Perhaps."

"I am empowered by my colleagues to negotiate a trade agreement beneficial to your friend...if he exists."

Poole sipped his double whiskey, frowning underneath the gray mustache.

"Such men are known to deal reluctantly with strangers. They prefer the company of trusted allies, and consult with unfamiliar tradesmen at a distance once removed."

"I understand. Unfortunately," Fowler said, "the quantities of cash and merchandise involved demand a more direct assurance from the source."

Poole's interest was apparent as he puffed on his cigar and asked, "What quantities are we discussing, Mr. Fraser?"

"Fifty kilos monthly at a price of twenty thousand per, with twelve months guaranteed. Twelve million dollars for the year. If your supplier wishes to continue the arrangement after one year's time, we can negotiate new terms in reference to the current market price."

"Your offer is extremely generous," said Poole. "Last month a kilo in Miami sold for sixteen-five on average."

"We're concerned about stability and reputation," Fowler said. "I grant you, we could save some money picking up a kilo here and there from amateurs. You also know the profit margin on cocaine, once it's been cut for resale on the street. My partners don't mind shaving pennies off their profit margin for a year or two if it will guarantee security and a dependable supply."

Poole smiled, revealing teeth like yellow Chiclets. "I believe there *is* a man with the connections you require. Dependability has always been his hallmark in the trade. Of course..."

"Is there a problem, Mr. Poole?"

"Security begins at home. My friend prefers to deal through intermediaries like myself. It helps him sleep at night."

"We all need sleep. It makes my partners nervous when their orders are misplaced or misinterpreted by go-betweens." He quickly raised a mollifying hand. "In most things, once the bargain was agreed on, I'm convinced they would be pleased to deal with someone like yourself, a man of honor and respect. But for the fine points of the deal itself..."

He left it hanging, Poole no longer angry or insulted, more concerned about potential loss of what could be a massive finder's fee for roping in a major customer to the Rodriguez family.

At last he said, "I would be derelict in my responsibility if I did not report your offer and allow the man I speak of to decide a course of action for himself." One hand slid down beside his chair. "As for the contents of this bag..."

"What bag?"

The yellow smile stretched ear to ear around the centerpiece of Poole's cigar. "My intuition tells me we shall be great friends."

"My second fondest wish is friendship," Fowler told him.

"And the first?"

"A lifetime of success in business, Mr. Poole."

"In Bahama, Mr. Fraser, they go hand in hand."

"In that case," Fowler raised his whiskey glass, "to friendship."

"To success."

"To love," said Weldon Glass, his face so somber that it made the others laugh out loud.

Inside, the redhead glanced out toward the balcony, saw three men laughing over business she would never understand, and turned back to her fashion magazine.

THEY MADE the short flight back in silence, cautious of the pilot and potential listening devices in the plane. When they were safely in the baby-blue Mercedes, rolling toward the Graycliff, Weldon Glass felt free to ask the question that was preying on his mind.

"You trust the man?"

"Hell no, do you?"

Glass frowned. "He may be satisfied with what he has."

"Not likely," Fowler said. "The normal finder's fee runs close to ten percent these days. Let's round it off and say a million dollars in his pocket if the deal goes through. That beats a hundred thousand any day."

"Ornelas may refuse."

"In that case, I'll be looking for another angle of attack. You have that conversation with your friend at Merchants Bank?"

"We spoke. I felt obliged to emphasize the risks involved."

"Don't do me any favors, guy."

"I won't."

"You know, if I get lucky with Ornelas and his boss, it just might help you with some basic cleanup on the local scene."

Glass shook his head, scowling. "The names mean nothing. If Rodriguez falls, another animal will take his place. The bureaucrats, from Poole to Pindling, will survive and draw their graft from those who wait in line."

"You feel like that, why stay? Turn in your shield, or find another place to practice."

"Bahama is my home," Glass said. "Police work is my life. I won't be driven off by leeches while I still have work to do."

Jack thought about Glen Keegan, saying pretty much the same damned thing when Fowler made his move to the DEA. A few years later, and Keegan was in the ground, his widow and his son alone.

"Are you a married man?"

"Two children," Glass replied. "Does that surprise you?"

Fowler shook his head. "Just curious. You watch your back, I guess."

"My back *and* front. In Nassau it's the only way to stay alive."

Upstairs, though it was barely lunchtime, Fowler felt an urge to bathe again. He compromised and washed his hands to scrub Poole's greasy touch away. He was emerging from the bathroom in his stocking feet and shirtsleeves when the telephone began to ring.

"Hello?"

"I am a friend of Weldon Glass."

It was a woman's voice, surprising Fowler, but he did not let it show.

"I'm glad you called."

"We have some business to discuss," she said. "Perhaps tonight."

"My place or yours?"

"Some neutral ground, I think. Say nine o'clock at the Calypso, Baillou Hill."

"I'll be there."

"Wear a flower in your buttonhole."

"What color?"

"White, for virtue's sake."

She severed the connection, cutting Fowler off before he had a chance to ask her name. The dial tone grated on his nerves until he cradled the receiver.

White, for virtue's sake.

A wild card now. He would have to watch himself from this point on. A woman changed the whole equation, even if he made believe that it was still the same.

"Goddamn it."

Desperate for that shower at last, he dropped his shoulder holster on the bed and started stripping off his clothes.

13

The white carnation didn't really match his suit, but Fowler followed orders. The Calypso lay a mile from his hotel, several blocks south of Government House on Baillou Hill Road. He drove the rental, found the night-club easily and parked beside the building in the L-shaped lot. The pulsing music came to meet him on the steps even before he reached the heavy double doors.

No hostess in a slinky gown this time. Instead a bouncer built like Mr. Universe accepted Fowler's five-dollar cover charge and passed him through without a second glance.

The music had been loud outside, but inside was bed-lam. Colored lights exploded like a fireworks show on the mirrored walls and ceiling, except that mere explosions would have been inaudible above the various strategic speakers blaring music from the stage.

The band was live, for what it might be worth—a kind of reggae-heavy metal blend that came on loud instead of passionate, discordant when it should have been intense. Jamaican accents made the lyrics damn near indecipher-able to Fowler, and the seven guys on stage were ob-viously high on something—ganja, coke, whatever—that relieved them of their minimal responsibility to put on a coherent show.

So much for art.

In spite of everything, the paying customers appeared to love it, many of them dancing with a style and energy that put the band to shame. From the expressions on their faces, some were out to get their money's worth no matter what, but most appeared to be enjoying their excursion on the wild side. There was marijuana in the air, mixed up with incense and perfume, but Fowler made no effort to identify its source.

Instead he navigated toward the bar, apologizing when the crush compelled close contact, mostly getting smiles and laughter in return. One dark-eyed sweetheart ran her fingers up his inseam, stroking Fowler, but she had no interest in his white carnation so he passed her by.

It was the kind of crowd you saw in movies, loose and loaded—both financially and chemically. He doubted if there were a dozen people in the room who could have passed a blood or breathalyzer test. At home he might have recognized some faces—politicians, people from the media, a kinky cop or two—but they were all blank slates to Fowler now. Inscrutable.

He did not even know who he was looking for...or more precisely, who was seeking him. A nameless, faceless woman, linked in some respect to Merchants Bank of Nassau. Age and race unknown. Her voice had sounded fairly young, but that could easily have been the telephone. No accent he could place, and yet...

Three-deep along the bar he finally caught the tender's eye and ordered Michelob on tap. It was not watered—first surprise—and Fowler was content to make it last, retreating to a nearby corner where the guys in charge had missed their chance to plant an amplifier, and the dancers rarely ricocheted within ten feet. He had a fair view of the entrance, bar and crowded dance floor, with the rest rooms just behind him on his right. At some point in the evening, Fowler reckoned everybody in the club would pass his vantage point at least one time.

In fact, it did not take that long. The woman found him moments later, as if she was watching from the time he entered, tracking him across the room and back again.

Jack saw her moving toward him on the fringes of the crowd, but did not focus on her face until she stopped in front of him and called him by his cover name.

"Would you be Mr. Fraser, then?"

He frowned. "I wore a white carnation, didn't I?"

"For virtue's sake, I think."

"You're Weldon's friend."

"Acquaintance. Prudence Sullivan."

He shook the hand she offered him and took the opportunity to size her up. She had high cheekbones, luminescent eyes, their shade concealed by the garish lighting, skin and curves that could have graced the cover of *Vogue* or *Cosmopolitan*—perhaps a *Playboy* centerfold if she was in the proper mood. The lady would have passed for lily-white in ninety-nine percent of Dixie's "private clubs," but Fowler saw a trace of native in her tan complexion, in the tight wave of her hair.

She had a drink already, something with a tiny parasol, so Fowler tried a different track. "Why don't we find a table, someplace we can talk?"

The lady shook her head, a galaxy of highlights in her hair.

"It's much too loud," she said. "I only had you meet me here so I could see you first. Make sure you came alone."

"You're satisfied?"

Her narrow smile was not without a touch of irony. "So far."

"I guess you have another place in mind?"

"I might, at that."

THE CALL from Weldon Glass had taken Prudence by surprise. They spoke no more than once or twice a month, and almost never on the telephone which they agreed should be reserved for bona fide emergencies. His mention of the tall American, together with a brief description of his mission, had been couched in terms that made it easy for her to refuse. The choice was hers in either case, and Weldon would not interfere.

She had agreed to meet the man on impulse—check him out at least—and find out for herself what kind of man he was. A decent judge of character, she came prepared to stand him up or tell him to his face that she would not involve herself, but here they were, emerging from the nightclub into semidarkness, shiny cars spread out before them in the parking lot.

Outside, away from all the smoke and noise, he asked her, "Do you have a car?"

"I took a cab."

"Mine's over here."

She fell in step beside him, feeling almost natural. She did not take to strangers readily, but there was something in his manner—a degree of confidence, perhaps—that made her feel at ease. He had a quiet strength about him that did not require intimidating gestures to reinforce it.

His car was tucked away behind the building in an angle of the parking lot where they were out of sight from the valets and bouncer on the door. With rented vehicles, she knew, the average tourist had a limited assortment to select from. He had managed to reserve a BMW, and his clothes said money, too—but Prudence understood that all of it might be a sham, the role he was assigned to play.

She hoped so, anyway.

Police with lots of money were, almost by definition, traitors to the badge.

The muggers seemed to come from nowhere, one emerging from between the two cars on her right, another stepping out in front of Fraser from the shadows on his left. Her ears picked up the footsteps of a third, behind them, but she balked at turning to confront the enemy.

"You smell like money," said the leader of the three, a scruffy black in denim shirt and jeans, with worn-out sandals on his feet.

The stranger smiled back and told him, "You've got a certain air yourself."

"A contribution for the poor man on the street?"

"Not likely, friend."

"But I am not your friend."

She didn't see the razor drawn. One moment Fraser's adversary stood before him empty-handed, and the next a tongue of glinting steel had sprouted from his fist. The man immediately on her right produced a folding knife, and Prudence heard a clinking sound behind her, conjuring the mental image of a chain.

"Your cash," the leader of the pack demanded. "And the woman's purse, right now."

"Well, since you put it that way..."

Her new acquaintance slid a hand inside his jacket, then brought it out again, the fingers wrapped around a lethal-looking automatic pistol. Prudence caught her breath, expecting sudden gunfire, but the tall American stepped forward, slashing with the muzzle of his gun, connecting with the nearest mugger and dropping him without a sound.

He had the others covered while Prudence slipped around behind him, edging toward the rental car. He handed her the key and stood his ground.

"You boys need practice," Fraser said. "Come up and see me in Miami sometime. I can introduce you to some guys who play this game for real. You ask them nice, they just might break you in...or maybe eat you up alive."

"We don't want trouble, mister," said the mugger with the knife.

"That so? I guess you're just some kind of butcher walking home from work, and you forgot to introduce yourself." As he spoke, he moved in closer to his prey, and when the mugger tried to answer, his foot came up between the legs with crushing force. The mugger fell on hands and knees, the blade forgotten as he tried to catch his breath.

"Two down," said Fraser, turning to the mugger who had dropped his chain and stood with hands limp at his sides. "You must be number three."

He raised the automatic, aiming, and the mugger bolted with a squeal of fright, abandoning his comrades to their fate. Watching from behind the wheel of Fraser's car, Prudence was relieved when he returned the pistol to concealment and slid in beside her on the rider's side.

"Your place or mine?" he asked. And smiled.

THEY MADE IT HERS, away from the hotel where someone might be watching Fowler's movements and logging any guests who came to call. Her flat was small but furnished in expensive taste, a three-room walk-up overlooking Soldier Road. She offered wine, but Fowler settled for a cup of coffee, freshly brewed.

The aftertaste of their encounter in the parking lot was unsettling, leaving Fowler with a moment of anxiety as he replayed the moves, the mugger's words, in search of any clue suggesting one—or both—of them had been set up. He did not trust coincidence, but strange shit happened all the time. He was relieved when Prudence Sullivan appeared to think no more about the incident and seemed prepared to let it go.

"You're interested in banking, I believe."

"I'm interested in certain customers at Merchants Bank, specifically."

"Which customers?"

"To start, Jorge Rodriguez, Rafael Ornelas and a slug named Ervin Steele."

"What makes you think that I can help you?"

"I assume our mutual acquaintance made that clear."

"He mentioned certain documents that might identify the owners of specific bank accounts. Of course, removal of such papers from the premises—much less delivery to outside hands—would be a violation of the law."

"I understand."

"Assuming I had access to these papers, Mr. Fraser... why should I assume such risk on your behalf?"

"No reason I can think of," Fowler said, "unless you're tired of watching people like Rodriguez and his toadies in the government move drugs through Nassau like there's no tomorrow. It doesn't help your country's reputation."

"In comparison to the United States, my country is an infant. We've been independent from the British crown for less than twenty years, and much of the corruption you observe in Nassau was inherited. Slaves learn by observation, Mr. Fraser. If corruption worries you so much, clean up Miami for a start."

"And how am I supposed to do that, when some fifty miles off-shore a so-called friendly nation rents its beachfront out to dealers? Your country may not be the source, but it's a big part of the current problem, and you know that. Half the poison on Miami streets stopped off in Bahama first to give your government a taste."

"We send you people, too," she said, a sudden, wistful tone encroaching on her voice. "My brother went to

Florida three years ago. To find his fortune in the Land of Opportunity.''

"So how'd he do?"

"He died. A drug deal, Mr. Fraser. Get rich quick. Except the deal went sour, and the buyer paid his debt off with a gun.''

"I'm sorry." Fowler meant it because he recognized her pain, but he had walked in on the same scenario a thousand times.

"I don't want sympathy," said Prudence Sullivan. "I want your understanding. If I help you now, it will not be for the United States, or even for my country. It is something that I owe my brother."

"Fair enough."

Her tears took Fowler by surprise. Embarrassed for a moment, he recovered quickly, moving closer on the couch and sliding one strong arm around her shoulders. Prudence clung to Fowler, weeping silently. He was uncomfortably conscious of her warmth beneath his hands, a stirring in himself that he could not control.

Long moments passed before she pulled away, slim fingers dabbing at her eyes, the tracks of moisture on her cheeks. "I'm sorry."

"Don't be. I know how it feels to lose someone you care about." He hesitated for a heartbeat, then finally went ahead. "Rodriguez killed a friend of mine not long ago, or had him killed. We weren't related, not like brothers, but it felt that way sometimes."

"It's personal for you, this business."

"Yes. It's personal."

She surprised him for the second time within five minutes, leaning in to kiss him softly on the lips. At first he hesitated to respond, arousal arguing inside his head with guilt and abstract visions of professional responsibility.

Arousal won.

She made no move to stop him when his fingers found the buttons of her blouse and slipped them open, one by one. She wore no bra, and Fowler cupped the supple roundness of her breasts, feeling the nipples stiffening against his palms. The silky fabric whispered as he slid it off her shoulders, leaving Prudence naked to the waist.

His coat and shoulder holster next, Jack's fingers felt clumsy as he started on the buttons of his shirt. She helped him, leaning in to kiss his chest and flick one nipple with her tongue before they got the shirttail out and Fowler could drop the garment on the floor.

They never made it to the bedroom. Fowler gently eased Prudence back against the couch and bent over her to catch one rigid nipple in his teeth. She tangled her fingers in his hair and drew his face against her flesh as Fowler's searching hands moved underneath her skirt. His fingers found the way, and Prudence muttered something unintelligible as he rolled bikini panties down her thighs and past her knees. He kicked his shoes off, wrestled off his slacks and joined her on the couch, with nothing in between them but the skirt bunched up around her waist. It made the moment sweeter, somehow, with the urgency of back-seat teenage coupling added as a dash of spice.

"Should I—"

"It's safe," she answered, reaching out for him and urging him inside.

Still, Fowler took the time to taste her, making Prudence squirm and thrust her hips against his face. He cupped her buttocks as he helped her reach the sweet relief she craved, then stayed with her as she got there, trembling, fingernails like talons digging into Fowler's scalp.

He rose and entered her before the tremors faded altogether, and his penetration brought her back, thighs

locked around his waist and pumping at him, matching
Fowler's rhythm with her own. She crossed her ankles,
heels against his coccyx, trapping him inside the liquid
heat of her. She nearly scalded him, but Fowler had no
thought of breaking free. He held himself above her,
back arched, elbows locked, enchanted by the flush that
had suffused her skin.

Her eyes came open for a heartbeat, meeting his and
holding there, before the lids came down again. She bit
her lip and shuddered, whimpering, and it was all too
much for Fowler. He descended on her, smothering her
face and slender neck with greedy kisses, moving down-
ward to the soft swell of her breasts, her nipples hard and
rough as pebbles on his tongue.

She bit his shoulder, sobbing, and he worked one hand
beneath her pumping buttocks, holding on with firm
possessiveness. She cried out at the sudden pressure,
taken by surprise, another climax rocking her as Fowler
let himself explode.

It's safe.

Her words, but even in the moment of release, Jack
Fowler knew that he was whistling past the graveyard,
flying in the face of death.

It was not safe by any means.

They lay together on the sofa afterward, and he could
feel her heartbeat like an echo of his own. Long moments passed before she stirred and found her voice.

"So tell me what you want."

14

Lieutenant Ervin Steele was a self-taught expert in damage control, defined in practical terms as the fine art of covering your ass. He had acquired the rudiments in childhood, growing up with parents who would hit first and ask questions later...if at all. The skill had been refined in boot camp, four years in the Corps, a turn at the police academy. In Metro-Dade Narcotics, you were covering your ass around the clock. It didn't matter if you had your hand out or you played it straight; whichever way it went, there was a world of hurt for careless cops around southern Florida these days.

But nothing in Steele's memory could match the past two days.

The second hit on Fowler was unauthorized, but Steele had made the choice to go ahead without approval from Rodriguez. It was chancy, knowing the Colombian, his stormy moods, but Steele knew *cops,* as well. He understood that taking off a lawman's partner was the same as murdering a family member—worse, if the surviving officer was short on next of kin. The fact that Fowler had moved on, became a Fed, meant nothing once that bond was formed. He kept in touch with Keegan, and the federal badge would only give him longer arms, more muscle in a crunch.

Which meant that he had to die.

Rodriguez would have come around in time and seen the common sense of taking Fowler out...assuming it had worked. The problem was, Steele's people blew it for the second time, and one of them was dumb enough to let himself get killed in the attempt.

Steele did not mourn Detective Stanley Hicks, per se. The boy was useful, with a mean streak that had come in handy several times, but if he stood next to Albert Einstein, no one would confuse them. In life, Hicks shied away from writing crime reports whenever possible because his spelling sucked, and he was rough on blacks and Cubans, even when he didn't need to be. If Stanley had a strong suit, it was guns, but even they had failed him in the parking lot at Billy Budd's.

It wasn't bad enough that he was linked with Ricky Kastor's near decapitation and a second failed attempt to kill a federal officer, but on top of that, the only decent shot Hicks made had killed a student from Miami-Dade J.C. and maimed his date, perhaps for life. The heat from IAD around Narcotics was intense, and it was all Lieutenant Steele could do to cover Stanley's tracks.

The other guys were hanging tough and playing dumb, despite the fact that Hicks had obviously not been flying solo on the raid. They managed to avoid incriminating evidence like fingerprints, thank God, and Fowler had not seen them well enough to finger anybody from the squad. The goons from IAD were linking Keegan's death with the attempt on Fowler, logically enough, and two dead cops prevented them from backing off until they had an explanation down in black and white.

Steele had a plan, if he could pull it off, but it would not be easy. He was thinking they could take advantage of the heat with Hicks and smear a little dirt on Keegan, make out like the two of them were working on a scam together when it blew up in their faces. Ricky Kastor's death could be a bonus if they played it right, because his presence at the scene allowed the introduction of civilians into the scenario. With any luck, Steele might turn up a cocaine cowboy he could sacrifice to demonstrate that Hicks and Keegan had been squeezing dealers on their own initiative. Once Keegan bought the farm, removed by Suspect X or his employees, Fowler had become a threat to Hicks, and Stanley had recruited gunners off the street to take him down.

It had potential, but it needed work.

And in the meantime, Ervin Steele had other problems on his mind. Like answering a summons from Jorge Rodriguez to the Blue Lagoon, close by Miami International.

It was the kind of place a boy might take his date if he had mischief on his mind. Another way to look at things, it made a halfway decent place for dumping bodies, if you did it properly. Most of them surfaced, for the simple reason that the killers were pathetic amateurs, but maybe one in every ten or twelve stayed down.

He stopped that line of thought. The trick was talking fast enough to get his story out before Rodriguez blew a fuse and had him iced. He might not have a chance, but it should count for something that he kept their date instead of cleaning out his safe-deposit box and running for his life. Rodriguez might respect his courage and allow him time to speak.

And if the bastard let him talk, Steele knew the odds were good that he would walk away.

Because he had a piece of information that Rodriguez needed now.

They needed one another to survive.

JORGE RODRIGUEZ watched a giant 747 lift off from the runway at Miami International, jet engines screaming as it powered over the expressway and the Blue Lagoon. It passed above him, blotting out the stars, and he imagined he was swimming underwater, glancing toward the surface where a killer shark was gliding, circling, knowing that its prey would have to rise and breathe.

He wondered how the peons stood it, living near the airport with its noise around the clock. Ten minutes waiting, and Rodriguez knew that he would crack before a single night went by.

There was a time in Medellín when he had slept out on the street or in dilapidated buildings of the city's meanest slum. The airport had been right downtown, before they built a new one to the north, and he had learned to sleep selectively—ignoring man-made thunder in the heavens, waking in a heartbeat to the sound of unfamiliar footsteps on his private turf.

These days Rodriguez slept in Coral Gables, miles removed from airport noise, and others were employed to stand guard in the night.

But he had not forgotten how to watch his back.

When there was trouble in the dealer's world these days, he studied causes and devised solutions, delegating the responsibility to his lieutenants and their soldiers on the street. A personal involvement multiplied his risk, and so Rodriguez saved himself for problems that he could not relegate to other hands.

Like now.

It galled him, having to repeat himself, but Ervin Steele had obviously failed to understand and carry out his orders in the present case. Instead of one policeman dead, they now had two—the second being one of *his*—along with various civilian casualties. Rodriguez had instructed Steele to leave the federal officer alone, and Steele had blatantly defied him. Worse, his men had botched the job.

Rodriguez knew the only cure for disobedience was punishment, but he had not decided on a penalty for Steele as yet. It would have pleased him to annihilate the clumsy bastard with his own two hands, but that would only mean another dead or missing cop and still more heat.

When things cooled down a bit, perhaps. But until then . . .

He saw the headlights of a car approaching, following the southern shore of the lagoon. Rodriguez did not have to speak or snap his fingers; the reaction from his soldiers was immediate and automatic. Four men took up their places by the one-lane road, a pair on either side. His driver stepped out and stood by the car, prepared to cover for Rodriguez if the shit came down.

Steele would be crazy to attempt a double cross in these conditions, but a spin around the television dial at news time was enough to show the countless crazy people in the world. Some of them put their babies in the microwave, and others ran for president. Some wore a badge and tried to pull shit on the man who *really* paid their salary.

His soldiers stopped the car with automatic weapons at the ready, shook Steele down and took his piece away before they let him pass, on foot. Rodriguez waited for him at the limo, making Steele do all the work.

"So, here we are."

The bastard was trying for a cocky attitude and missing by a fraction, like a clinker on a baby grand. Rodriguez smiled at him and said, "It's lucky you could find this place, the fucked-up way you follow my directions."

"Wait a second, now—"

"*You* wait, *pendejo*. I gave orders you should leave the goddamn Fed alone. Specifically I told you do not hit the man. You understand my English pretty good?"

"Jorge—"

"I'm thinking maybe you got problems with your hearing. Something in your ears, could be. I think one of my doctors here should bore 'em out with a .357."

"Can I tell you something?" Steele was sweating, but he was on his feet. "You want to whack me anyway, some last words couldn't hurt."

"You got one minute, asshole."

"Fowler isn't someone you can deal with like a normal guy. I pulled his file, okay? The prick's straight-arrow, like his partner, Keegan. You remember Keegan? He's the one was bleeding in your living room."

"Smart off to me, I'll cut your lips off, stick 'em up your ass."

"In that case, I won't have a chance to tell you Fowler had the operation made before I tried the second hit. You'll never hear that he was asking questions down at Metro-Dade and running tracers back to you on Keegan's death."

"The guy's got squat. He's nothing."

"He's a Fed who won't let go, since someone blew his partner up. You think he's sitting on his hands right now, all worried someone tried to kill him twice? I don't suppose you give a rat's ass where he is?"

"You want to tell me something, spit it out."

"He's *gone,*" Steele said. "I don't mean running, I mean *hunting.* In the islands."

"What the hell . . . ?"

"Don't thank me yet. I pulled some strings downtown, found out the federal shooting board already cleared him on the splash at Billy Budd's. That's no surprise. The fun part is, he's not back on the street. A guy like that, he should be working overtime to find the guys who iced his partner and tried to dust him twice. If it was me, I'd pitch a tent at Metro-Dade and watch the uniforms go by, see any of them acting hinky when they catch my scent."

"You said the islands."

"So I had to ask myself, if Fowler's gone, where would he go? Vacation? Disneyworld?" Steele shook his head. "Guy's looking for a way to tie the loose ends up around your neck before he gets his ass shot off. The one place he can maybe sneak around and do a job, where no one knows his face."

"In Nassau?"

"Bingo. Pay the man."

"I think you're blowing smoke."

"So give the word. Your boys have got my piece. I figure there's enough of them to do the job all right."

"If Fowler's on the island, what's his game?"

"I never promised I could read his mind. Offhand, I couldn't even tell you what he calls himself when he goes under."

"Then—"

"I've got his picture, though."

Steele held the glossy snapshot up in two fingers, like a slick mechanic showing off his hold card on a winning hand. Rodriguez took it from him staring at the earnest face. He saw a man who would not bend, determination in his eyes.

"I lifted that from Fowler's jacket, down in personnel. He's got a few miles on him, since they took that snap, but if your people on the island have a decent pair of eyes between them, they should run him down in no time. Look for someone trying to fit in. Not like a tourist, necessarily. A player, looking for the game."

"For your sake, Steele, this better not be shit. If I scramble troops on Nassau, I don't want to see your man turn up around Fort Lauderdale, or anywhere at all."

"I trust my hunches."

"Good. You bet your life on this one."

"Fair enough."

"It's more than fair," Rodriguez told him, tight-lipped. "You're breathing, after you defied my orders once. Next time I call you up and say go take a crap in front of city hall at noon, you better be there with your pants around your ankles."

"Sure. Okay."

"Yes, sir."

Steele plainly had it in his mind to balk at that, but real survivors know which asses they must kiss to get along.

"Yes, sir."

"We're finished now."

Steele nodded, gratefully retreating toward his car. The soldiers gave his pistol back and kept him covered as he drove away, while Rodriguez stood in the darkness by the Blue Lagoon, holding a snapshot of a dead man in his hand.

The only trouble was, the dead man didn't know it yet.

Someone would have to clue him in without delay.

THE LAST THING Rafael Ornelas needed in the middle of the night was trouble reaching out to grab him by the neck and boot him in the ass. Despite his reputation as a brawler and a triggerman, he liked things smooth and easy where the money was concerned. If there was one thing he had learned by following Jorge Rodriguez on the rocky road from Medellín to Nassau, it was plain old, everyday arithmetic.

Cocaine plus honest lawmen equaled heat.

And heat was bad for business, no matter how you looked at it.

Ornelas knew that there were many different ways to deal with heat before your house caught fire. If you were hassled by a cop you couldn't buy, you flipped a coin.

Come heads, you set your sights a little higher, buy his boss off—or his boss's boss, whatever was required; come tails, you snuff the bastard out and risk *more* heat to find a permanent solution for your problem at the source.

In his younger days he would have hoped for tails, a chance to see some action and eliminate a cop, regardless of the risk. But he'd become an older, somewhat wiser man of means, and Ornelas always tried the silver first, before he turned to lead.

Well . . . *almost* always.

The exception to his rule was undercover men, who wormed their way inside an operation like a maggot tunneling through meat and tried to eat you from the inside out. A guy like that, you couldn't reason with him, put his kids through college for him like you could an ordinary narc. Ornelas thought of undercover spies as germs; you either killed them off, or you got sick and died yourself.

The night Rodriguez called him at his home on Paradise, Ornelas was relaxing in his hot hub and enjoying the view of Nassau Harbor, with an attentive blonde by his side. The last thing Rafael looked forward to was Hector Bustamonte standing there and holding out a telephone, informing him it was Rodriguez on the line.

He sent the blonde away to have a swim in the pool nearby. Cool water made her nipples perky, and it made him smile to watch her splashing in the shallow end.

Then he took the telephone from Hector, and Rodriguez wiped his smile away, and along with it, his desire.

The notion of an undercover DEA man working Nassau came as no surprise, but this one had a different smell about him. He was motivated by a private grudge, and they had missed him twice around Miami, when they should have nailed his ass and hung him out to dry.

Trust dirty cops to fuck up everything they touched.

Ornelas sat and listened to his orders after sending Hector back inside to man the fax machine. A photo of their man was on the way, and Rafael would take the ball from there.

A touchdown, all the way.

When Rodriguez hung up, Ornelas left the hot tub, dripping along the deck, a squat man striding naked toward the house. The blonde called out to him, but he ignored her. It was strictly business now.

And business worried Rafael Ornelas at the moment.

He was sitting on a brand-new offer for a multimillion-dollar deal, and suddenly he knew that it was going sour. There was no way he could prove that Gorman Poole was playing footsie with a ringer yet, but once he had the photograph in hand . . .

Goddamn it, anyway.

The deal had sounded sweet, as Poole explained it. Too damned sweet to fly. You had to figure that with a thing that perfect on the surface there was something rotten underneath.

Of course, he could be wrong. The dealer from Miami—Jason Fraser—might not be the undercover narc who meant to bring Rodriguez down, and everyone around him. The coincidence of timing might be nothing more than that, a mere coincidence.

But Rafael would have to clear it up and be certain of his facts before he went ahead. It would be bad enough, a fucking narc that close to Poole and maybe sending back reports to the United States, without a face-to-face that tied in Ornelas.

Still carrying the cordless telephone, he tapped Poole's private number out from memory. It rang six times before the sleepy bastard answered, sounding like a junkie on the downside of his ride.

"Get dressed," Ornelas ordered when he knew the man was awake. "Somebody will be waiting when you get downstairs."

"What is it, Rafael?"

"I'll give you fifteen minutes. Move your ass."

A twenty-minute hop from Grand Bahama in the helicopter, and by that time Poole would be alert enough to view the snapshot, tell him whether he had ever seen the federal agent's face before.

In Freeport, for example, talking deals.

If Gorman made a match, it would be time to move.

The only problem with a burial at sea was how to keep your feet dry while you dug the grave.

15

The morning after, Fowler woke in his hotel room, wondering if he was blown. He had not spent the night with Prudence Sullivan, but they made love a second time before he left, when he had finished spelling out his needs and Prudence had agreed to help.

So far, so good...unless the lady was a ringer, playing Weldon Glass along and putting out a phony line about her late, lamented brother in the States.

It was a possibility, of course, but Fowler didn't buy it. As a judge of character, he ranked himself among the best, and he had grown adept at spotting liars from a distance. It seemed improbable that he and Glass would both be taken in—especially when the man from ISD appeared to have no special interest in the woman—but Fowler knew enough to watch his every step on hostile ground.

If Prudence found the documents he needed and delivered them on time, he would be halfway home. If she tried to set him up...well, there were ways to cope with that eventuality when the time arrived.

He wanted to believe in Prudence, and the wanting was a danger sign—an indicator of potential blind spots—but Fowler had to place his trust in someone, sometime. On his own, without an ally in the world, he would be nothing but a one-man vigilante force, predestined for annihilation by his enemies.

His trust did not extend to hotel telephones. The room might not be bugged, but there were many ways to eavesdrop on a conversation. A switchboard operator could be bribed, or taps could be installed at any point between the handset and the trunk line, miles away. In any case, the end result would be the same: his cover blown, his life in jeopardy.

When he had showered, dressed and finished breakfast in his room, Jack went downstairs and made his exit through the lobby, past the parking lot and onto West Hill Street. He traveled north on foot, with the casual interest of a tourist window shopping, pausing now and then to see if anyone did likewise in his wake. When he was reasonably certain that he had no tail, he picked up speed and started looking for a public telephone.

He found one at a shopping center, half a mile from his hotel.

Some governments routinely monitored the public telephones within their jurisdiction, hoping for a tidbit of subversive conversation on the line, but Fowler doubted whether Pindling's crew could handle such an operation even if they felt the need. Half-turned so he could watch the street, he dialed a number for the federal building in Miami, made the call collect and smiled as Rudy Stano grudgingly accepted charges on the other end.

"You sound a little out of sorts this morning, Rudy."

"Getting there. I've got a huddle with some geek from OMB at noon. What's new with you?"

"We're cooking. I've got feelers out to meet with Jorge's number two and close a major deal, ASAP. The flip side, there's a possibility I may have found myself some eyes inside the Merchants Bank."

"It couldn't hurt."

"We still have paper out on Rafael Ornelas?"

"Last I heard. It's been a couple years since anybody saw him in the States, but they were looking for him on a murder warrant out of Tampa."

"If my luck holds, I'll be talking to him pretty soon. I'll try and cut a deal where payment is contingent on delivery around the Keys somewhere. First time around, he makes a good-faith personal appearance and we drop a net."

"That simple?"

"I sincerely hope so."

"IAD's been stirring up the dust at Metro-Dade and getting nowhere since you left. I'm hearing talk that Hicks and Keegan had some kind of action going down with Ricky Kastor, and it went sour."

Fowler felt the heat of anger rising in his cheeks. "That's bullshit. I had Kastor on the line to dig up anything he could on Steele and company. The bastards used him when they set me up."

"I *know* that, Jack. You ought to know what's being said, is all. Unless we nail Rodriguez and his bluesuits pretty quick, I have a sneaking hunch they'll find a pile of 'evidence' somewhere to show your guy was dirty."

"I'm on top of it," he said.

"Make sure you stay that way. A deal like this rolls over on you, you'll be in a world of hurt."

"I like your confidence."

"Hey, Jack, it's not *my* confidence you have to think about. Rodriguez has the islands sewn up tight—or *thinks* he does. You rock the boat down there, and somebody's bound to try and make you walk the plank."

"I brought my water wings."

"A hungry shark eats anything, I hear."

"Good luck with OMB."

"I'm thinking I should squirt the guy with Preparation H. Might shrink him down to size. Stay frosty, will you?"

"It's the only way to fly."

The anger was a tool he could use if he controlled it, storing up the nervous energy for a moment when he needed something extra, a surprise advantage. It sharpened his senses, made him more alert, intent on finishing the game.

He was too late to save Glen Keegan's life and spare his family the pain of loss, but maybe Fowler still had time to save his partner's reputation if he played his cards exactly right. A fumble now and he was history.

Like Glen.

And did it really matter what a bunch of vultures said or thought about the dead?

Damn right.

No longer caring if he had a tail, Jack Fowler turned and started back toward the hotel.

ALONE WITH THE COMPUTER, Prudence Sullivan worked magic. She had stayed behind when other members of the staff at Merchants Bank went out to lunch, claiming she was tied up with paperwork that could not wait. In fact, the urgency was real, but she was busy searching confidential records for the names and corresponding numbers of selected key depositors.

She was not cleared officially for access to the data she required, but she had managed to obtain a copy of the entry code that morning, bending over the assistant manager's desk with a trivial question, trading him a glimpse of creamy cleavage for a password swiftly memorized. He never knew the difference, and with any kind of luck, no one would ever know that she had accessed private files without permission from the management.

She felt a bit like Mata Hari, or the good girl in a James Bond movie, risking everything she had to find a crucial bit of evidence against the enemy.

In fact, she thought the risk was more illusory than real. The confidential files were "sealed" with mandatory access codes, but they maintained no record of perusal if the operator failed to log one in. Unless somebody caught her in the act, they would be none the wiser, powerless to stop her from delivering the evidence to Jason Fraser when they met again.

The thought of him produced a storm of contradictory emotions, leaving Prudence momentarily distracted and confused. Her physical reaction to the man had been unusual in itself, but there was more. He was a stranger, really, and she knew they had no future, but she felt compelled to help him all the same. Her brother, Thomas, was a part of it, no doubt...but she was also helping Jason on her own behalf.

To clear her conscience of implicit guilt? Because she recognized a link between her brother's death and the "respectable" depositors she dealt with every day?

She had begun her tenure at the Merchants Bank as a lowly teller, logging in deposits and withdrawals from a cage downstairs, remembering to smile and thank each customer in turn as cash changed hands. Promotion came with time and study, but she knew the kinds of people she was dealing with before a month was out. Their clothes and jewelry, flashy cars and lurking bodyguards, told Prudence everything she had to know.

Of course, the bank had law-abiding patrons, too—the merchant class from which its name was drawn—and while they constituted a majority in terms of numbers, Prudence quickly learned that their deposits added up to something like one-third of the cash on hand. At Merchants Bank, investments ran primarily toward foreign loans with interest well below prime...in short, a classic money laundry, washing income from the traffic in illicit drugs.

Her brother had observed the smiling men with their expensive jewelry, flashy suits and chauffeured limousines, aspiring to a place among their ranks. He asked around the streets and quickly found out that the action happened in Miami, less than eighty miles away. It was a relatively simple thing to save his money for a round-trip airline ticket, thinking to himself that he would never need the passage home.

As it happened, he was right.

The details were obscure, but Prudence learned that he was working as a mule, transporting packages for men who paid in cash and carried guns. The night he died, some other men were waiting for him when he left a cheap hotel with a shoe box swathed in tape and wrapping paper tucked beneath his arm. The box contained narcotics, and the waiting men were not police.

He might have lived if he had maintained his cool and simply given up the package on demand. It struck her that he might have been afraid of his employers, of some reprisal if he lost the load, but she would never know.

The brutal facts remained. He ran, and there was shooting. Thomas bled to death before the ambulance arrived. No package was recovered at the murder scene.

She had no evidence connecting any of the customers at Merchants Bank with what had happened to her brother in Miami. It was possible that she had met his killers, or at least the man who paid their salaries, but Prudence did not let the question prey upon her mind. Instead she told herself that her brother had been foolish, reckless. He had thrown his life away, but life went on for others.

She had work to do, and she was doing it today.

If Jason Fraser used the information she supplied to take a dealer off the streets, he would be saving lives. His motive of revenge was unimportant; in the end, it meant no more than hers.

It might not be correct to say ends justified the means, but there was something to be said for justice in the raw. A breach of ethics and a violation of the banking law on her part might save someone else's brother from a firing squad in Florida, New Orleans or Atlantic City.

It was worth the risk.

She found what she was looking for at 12:19, the first of two names Fraser had provided, with the corresponding number for a bank account. The second name and number flashed across the screen eleven minutes later, and she spent a moment printing out the data on a scroll of perforated paper, ripping off the pages that she needed and disposing of the rest. A simple cross-check gave her monetary totals as of the previous day. Another moment with the whirring printer and her work was done.

She folded up the printouts, hid them in her purse, then pressed a key to scrub the confidential files. Unless someone should find the papers in her bag, they had no way of proving she had ever cracked the access code to scan the private list of names.

Her stomach growled, reminding her that the hour reserved for lunch was almost gone. No matter. She had missed a meal or two before, and she could always grab a candy bar from the dispenser outside her office cubicle if it came down to that.

Abandoning the terminal, she thought of Jason Fraser, wondered how he would react when she delivered the material he needed. Would he leave for the United States at once, or could she talk him into staying for a day or two and enjoy his company in partial payment for a job well done?

She passed a group of secretaries in the hallway who were coming back from lunch, relieved that they had not been moments earlier. With the danger behind her now, she felt deflated, like an athlete who had burned up every ounce of strength to reach the finish line ahead of her competitors.

And something else. A small sense of achievement warming her inside.

For Thomas.

For herself.

THE TELEPHONE WAS midway through its second ring when Fowler answered.

"Mr. Fraser?"

"Speaking."

"Do you recognize my voice?"

"Of course." One did not easily forget the dulcet tones of Gorman Poole.

"A friend of mine is interested in meeting you to talk about a business proposition."

"Excellent."

"He is available this evening at the hour of ten o'clock."

"Suits me."

"A driver will collect you. Shall we say at half-past nine?"

"I'll meet him on the street."

"A white Mercedes-Benz."

"Is Weldon coming?"

"That will not be necessary, Mr. Fraser. He has served his purpose, as it were. From now on you shall deal with me."

"That's progress, eh?"

"Until this evening."

There was dead air on the line as Poole broke the connection, Fowler cradling the handset with a frown. It stood to reason Glass would not be with him all the way, but he could still have used some backup for the meeting with Ornelas. There was nothing to suggest a setup, but when you were dealing with a crowd like this, you never knew.

Eight hours.

He could try to get in touch with Prudence Sullivan before the meet, but it was risky, taking chances with a tail. If they spoke in guarded terms, he could afford to call her, and she could tell him if her check of the computer files had been successful. Still, she would not be off work for hours yet, and he had time to kill.

He finally opted for a walk downtown to give himself some exercise and work off the accumulated tension. He could have a drink or two, be back in ample time for dinner and a call to Prudence from his room before he had to meet Poole's driver.

From that point on, it would be anybody's game.

If Rafael Ornelas took the bait, there would be business to discuss and further meetings to arrange. It would be tricky, setting up the stage for Rafael to make the first delivery himself on U.S. soil, but Fowler knew that Rudy Stano was prepared to pay if necessary from the built-up store of confiscated funds. There was a special irony—poetic justice—in using one thug's cash to put another in the bag.

Ornelas would be facing Murder One if they could get him back to Tampa, and he had to know that Florida was one of half a dozen states where executions still continued with a kind of clockwork regularity. A glimpse of the electric chair—"Old Sparky" to prospective occupants—might be enough to loosen his tongue.

And if Ornelas started singing, naming names, the DEA could nail Rodriguez down without delivering his case to the IRS for income tax evasion or some other penny-ante charge. If Rafael caved in, Rodriguez would be doing major time before the year was out.

If he didn't . . . well, with Prudence Sullivan's assistance and the data out of Merchants Bank, they had a chance to put a painful crimp in Jorge's style. His "clean" accounts in Florida were good for several million at the very least, and everything he purchased with his money—cars and houses, boats and diamond rings, airplanes and real estate—would be up on the auction block if they could make the crucial Nassau link.

Emerging from the hotel lobby into brilliant sunshine, with the fragrance of the gardens all around, Jack Fowler tried to put the problem out of mind. The next eight hours were his own to spend or squander as he liked, and fretting over possibilities would do no good for anybody in the end.

He reached the street, turned left and started to retrace that morning's circuit. Letting down his guard a trifle, Fowler did not bother checking for a tail.

Two gunners fell in step behind him, hanging back a block or so and keeping pace. They knew their man from photographs they carried, but they made no move to intercept.

No hurry, now.

They had all day to do it right.

16

He made the gunmen coming out of a boutique on Mackey Street by the too casual way they stood together on a nearby corner, smoking cigarettes and checking out the action from behind their Foster Grants. One of them caught a glimpse of Fowler just emerging from the shop, and he snapped his head around too quickly, trying to avoid the obvious. They could have passed for bookends in their tropic suits with hardware underneath, white shoes, long hair that hung in greasy tangles past their collars.

He spent a moment in the shaded doorway, scouting out the street in each direction, spotting one more look-alike directly opposite, perusing the display of pipes at a tobacco shop. If there were three on foot, he had to figure they had wheels nearby, at least one other man to drive the car and perhaps some infantry he couldn't see.

Continuing along his way, he felt the troops fall into step behind him. Fowler's mind was racing, trying to determine whether he was merely being watched or set up for the kill.

He knew that Gorman Poole had spoken to Ornelas, and their meet—supposedly—was set for ten o'clock that night. Of course, the call and scheduled rendezvous could be a ruse, designed to throw him off his guard and make him careless in the face of a prospective million-dollar deal. Relaxed, he made an easy target for the enemies who posed as friends.

There were alternatives, and Fowler thought about them as he traveled north on Mackey toward the harbor

front. Protective cover was a possibility, surveillance ordered by Ornelas to insure his unknown future business
partner was not rubbing elbows with police or holding
court with members of a rival syndicate before they met
to talk a deal. It made a fair amount of sense, but three
men on a simple shadow job seemed like overkill to
Fowler.

Another possibility included rival dealers looking for
an easy score. In Nassau, as in Miami, rip-offs were a
constant threat to smuggling operations, large or small.
The walls might not have ears, but every drug cartel and
government department had its share of leaks, where
major money was concerned. The satchel he had passed
to Gorman Poole would be enough to put the jackals on
his scent; the rumor of a multimillion-dollar payoff down
the road could start a feeding frenzy in the pack.

Before he reached the harbor front at Potter Cay, Jack
knew that he would have to check it out and lose the tail,
no matter who had put the gunners on his track. If they
were merely watching him, it would not hurt to send Ornelas back a message, showing him that Fowler dealt
from strength. If they were looking for a place to make a
hit, his only recourse lay in striking first, assuming the
advantage of surprise.

The Nassau Yacht Haven was coming up on his left.
From the sidewalk, tourists were snapping pictures of the
ships and the owners in their nautical regalia. Fowler
thought about the clubhouse, then finally decided it was
too much hassle and continued on his way. His shadows
held their place some twenty yards behind him, one remaining on the far side of the street in case he veered
across.

Fort Montagu was just ahead, also teeming with tourists, but at least the setting gave him room to move. He
killed ten minutes ambling around the fort, overlooking

the sea gardens and Paradise Island from its parapets before he ducked inside a public rest room.

One man was standing at a urinal, and the first of half a dozen stalls was occupied. Jack took the second one in line and left the door unlatched behind him, stepping on the toilet seat and crouching down so that his feet would not be visible below. He had the automatic in his hand before the outer door creaked open and he heard two sets of footsteps on the tile.

The urinal was flushed; somebody started running water in a sink. The exit whispered open, shut. A shadow moved along the line of toilet stalls, confirming one stool occupied.

At first the knock was soft enough to be confused with something else. Jack heard the man beside him shifting on his toilet seat, distracted from the task at hand.

"You want to try the next one, please?"

Instead of backing off, one gunner started kicking at the metal door with enough force to rattle the partition separating Fowler from the target stall. His decoy started snatching toilet paper off the roll and fumbling with his slacks, but he was too damned slow. A third kick broke the flimsy latch and slammed the door wide open with a bang.

Jack made his move, emerging from the second stall as his pursuers gaped in wonder at the stranger's face. The man before them had his pants around his ankles, both hands covering his lap. There was no color in his face as his eyes locked upon the pistols his assailants held.

Behind them, Fowler braced the Glock in a two-handed grip, prepared for anything.

And said, "You lose."

They knew enough to freeze, relaxing trigger fingers as they craned their necks to stare. One of them curled his lip, about to speak, but Fowler never let him get that far.

"The pistols first," he said. "Be careful when you hand them to my friend."

The gunners stared at Fowler, blinked at one another, finally passed their weapons to the pale man on the toilet. Modest to a fault, he kept his right hand firmly planted where it was, accepting first one piece and then the other with his left. They clattered as he dropped them on the floor.

"Toward me, make it backward," Fowler ordered. Suiting words to action, he retreated toward the line of sinks, his captives shuffling backward after him. He knew that he was running out of time before the third man wandered in to find out what was keeping his companions.

"On your knees."

They knelt reluctantly, a foot or so apart. When Fowler struck the first one hard behind one ear with his pistol, the gunner toppled forward on his face. His sidekick twisted awkwardly and lunged at Fowler, catching him around the legs, the momentum driving Fowler back against the sinks.

The goddamned guy was biting him, teeth gouging at his thigh, when Fowler brought the pistol down across his skull. The first blow opened up his scalp with a spurting of blood but it took three more to drop him on the tile. No time to check for vital signs, and Fowler frankly did not give a damn.

He slipped the pistol in a pocket of his coat, and as he left the rest room, he met the other gunman coming in. The shooter made him, digging for a weapon underneath his arm, and Fowler had no options left. He drew and shot his adversary in the chest from seven feet away. The impact dropped Mr. X before he had a chance to reach his gun.

So much for sublety.

A woman screamed somewhere behind him, and he ran. He was expecting panic, possibly pursuit, but the explosion of a gunshot on his flank took Fowler by surprise. He ducked and pivoted in that direction, quick enough to spot a fourth torpedo sighting down the barrel of chrome revolver and squeezing off another round.

Jack threw himself behind a green oil drum that had been converted to a trash can, and from there dodged behind a concrete bench. A bullet chipped the masonry and ricocheted among the tourists, touching off another round of screams.

He risked a glance along the line of fire and saw that there were two men closing on him, breaking off in opposite directions with a classic pincer move. Around them, men and women scattered in confusion, running aimlessly for cover, spoiling Fowler's shot. His enemies, by contrast, blazed away without compunction, and he saw a teenage girl go down before the gunner on his left, blood spurting from her face.

He broke from cover, leading them away, a bullet whipping past his shoulder as he ran. The next round clipped a fat man to the left and whirled him like a top, his expensive camera gear demolished when it hit the pavement.

Fowler spun around into a fighting crouch, the Glock extended, sighting down the slide. He caught the gunner on his right flat-footed, in the clear, and squeezed off two quick shots from twenty feet. The first round struck his adversary just above the belt line, blotting crimson on his shirt. The second went in higher, near the collarbone, and pitched him over backward in a sprawl.

The other man was firing at him now, and Fowler felt his jacket ripple as a bullet plucked the hem. He dodged aside and kept on going, through a shoulder roll that jarred his teeth together, coming up on one knee, both hands on his gun.

A woman ran in front of his assailant, and the gunman sent her reeling with a vicious backhand, sacrificing aim to vent his rage. For just a heartbeat he was open, arms spread wide, and Fowler took advantage of the moment, squeezing off one well-placed round. The bullet struck his target in the upper chest and ripped on through, blood spouting as he fell.

Fowler ran across the sloping lawn and back in the direction of the street. Police would be arriving any moment, and he had to put the park behind him while he had the chance. No time for questions yet, before he found out if Ornelas was responsible for the attack.

Ahead of him, he saw the traffic stalled at curbside, drivers leaning on their horns or pulling out to pass a dark sedan in the outside lane that crept along by inches. Three men were inside the car, and while he did not recognize their faces, one of them was pointing at him, saying something to the others with a note of urgency.

He saw the weapons then, an Uzi and a riot gun protruding from the rider's side. He cursed and veered off course, had barely time enough to fling himself behind a tree before the gunners opened fire. A storm of parabellum rounds and buckshot ripped the bark above him, stray rounds gouging divots in the grass. Up range, unlucky tourists scattered, several of them going down before the first barrage.

The hit car had completely stopped by now, ignoring traffic as the passengers unloaded in a rush. Deprived of options, Fowler poked his gun around the tree and squeezed off four quick rounds, his nearest target dropping prone but seemingly unharmed. Another shotgun blast kicked dust in Fowler's face as he retreated out of range.

He heard the sirens coming from a distance, somewhere near the heart of town. The traffic would delay them, but he could not count on any extra time. A burst of automatic fire chewed up the grass on Fowler's right, reminding him that he was trapped.

Without a conscious plan, he rose behind the tree and caught a sturdy branch above his head. With a twisting lunge, Fowler hooked one leg across the limb, then straddled it, his muscles cracking from the strain. Unable to release the Glock, he had to do it all one-handed, and he had to make it work the first time out.

The price of failure was his life.

Another shift, and Fowler had an elevated view of one assailant on his right. It was the shotgun, squeezing off another blast that scorned the trunk a yard beneath his feet. The guy was on his feet, a perfect silhouette at twenty paces, when the Glock spat three quick rounds and cut him down.

The Uzi had him pegged then, hacking random patterns on the bark as Fowler kicked back into free-fall, dropping to the earth below. The impact jarred him, emptying his lungs, but he had strength enough to swing his piece around and lock on target, letting need and instinct guide his aim.

He caught the gunner firing upward, toward the canopy of leaves above his head, and fired off two quick rounds before the enemy had time to recognize his last mistake. One missed, but he was satisfied with number two, a groin shot, staggering the shooter with a cry of pain.

The Uzi kept on firing, clutched in spastic hands, the muzzle jerking aimlessly and spewing parabellum rounds across the lawn. Another slug from Fowler's automatic caught him in the shoulder, spinning him around, his last few bullets lost in traffic, chipping paint from passing cars.

Another round between his shoulder blades toppled him, then Jack recovered sufficiently to rise and face the hit car in a combat shooter's stance. The driver saw death coming for him, and he ducked below the dash, tires screeching as he jumped the curb and ran for half a block with two wheels on the sidewalk, two wheels on the grass, before he cut back into traffic at the nearest intersection.

Fowler let him go, the sirens sounding closer now as he ran south on Village Road. It was the long way back to his hotel, but his priority was making tracks, acquiring distance from the unexpected battleground.

He tucked the automatic out of sight and slowed his pace deliberately, looking like a slightly rumpled tourist and merging with the flow of passersby. After two blocks, he began to think that he had pulled it off, no witnesses on hand to point him out or summon the police.

Above all else, he needed time to think. It seemed to Fowler that the hit had been too organized, too many men involved for any kind of simple rip-off. He was not in a position to interrogate his enemies, the ones he left alive, but the attack had been too brazen for a minor gang of hoodlums to attempt.

Which left Ornelas, acting for Rodriguez, or an unknown set of big-league players jumping in the game.

He reached the Graycliff sweaty and exhausted, looking forward to a shower and a change of clothes. The desk clerk blinked at Fowler as he passed, surprised by grass stains on his pants and jacket, but he kept his observations to himself and settled for a bland "Good afternoon."

Jack's legs were aching as he hit the stairs, but he refused to slow his pace. He thought about the shower, and decided that he might prefer a nice hot bath. A chance to soak and let his mind drift free, examining the meager evidence at hand.

His key turned in the lock too easily. The door, already open, shifted slightly at his touch. Instead of bolting, Fowler stood his ground and nudged it further with his foot. A wedge of room swung into view, expanding to reveal a black man in a business suit.

The stranger in his room was flanked by uniforms.

Police.

He did not feel like running anymore. If they had traced him here, the game was up—or part of it, at least. They might not know about the shooting yet. If they were looking for a handle on Rodriguez and his crew, the visit might turn out to be routine. In any case, he had to act as natural as his appearance would permit.

"What's going on?" he asked, across the threshold now, a mix of curiosity and indignation in his tone.

The suit regarded him with frank suspicion. "Jason Fraser?"

"Right. You want to tell me what you're doing in my room?"

He missed the signal, if there was one, but the uniform on Fowler's right stepped forward, swinging from the basement with a fist that struck Fowler in the solar plexus and dropped him to his knees. Somebody grabbed his jacket at the collar, pulled it down and back to pin his arms, and someone else removed his pistol from the shoulder rig.

"Stand up."

When he did not comply at once, rough hands gripped Fowler's arms and dragged him to his feet. The suit was in his face, with breath that smelled like cinnamon.

"There are important questions you must answer, Mr. Fraser. You will come with us."

"I want to call the U.S. embassy," he said when he could find his voice.

"In time, perhaps. For now, you are in no position to be giving orders. *I* decide your rights and privileges."

It was the suit who punched him, smiling with a kind of brittle charm. Jack saw it coming this time, tried to tense his stomach muscles but the fist exploded in his groin. They held him upright when his legs gave way, and Fowler clenched his teeth against the waves of nauseating pain.

Eyes closed, he missed the blackjack as it rose and fell, connecting with his skull. Behind his eyelids, colored sparks erupted in a light show that was instantly eclipsed by darkness, plunging into midnight depths beyond the reach of pain or conscious thought.

17

The pain was waiting when he came around, a throbbing in his skull and lower down, his torso alternately numb and aching. Waves of dull, insistent agony tied his stomach up in knots. A taste of vomit in his mouth told him he had nothing left to give.

Full consciousness returned by slow degrees. He was aware of sitting naked—no, he still had shorts on—in a straight-backed wooden chair. The handcuffs on his wrists were almost tight enough to cut circulation in his fingers, and Fowler flexed them to bring sensation back. His ankles had been manacled as well, using two pairs of cuffs against the front legs of the chair.

There were bright lights above him, but the room was cool from air-conditioning. When Fowler opened his eyes, chin resting on his chest, he had a view of concrete floor. Three feet in front of him was a metal grate above a drain.

Jack closed his eyes again, remembering. A shootout in the park with five men hit, at least. How many dead? Police already waiting for him at the Graycliff, slugging him unconscious in his room. The memory revived pain he had forgotten, in his ribs and groin.

He was not at the Graycliff now. Without examining the room or giving any other sign that he was conscious, Fowler recognized the crude interrogation chamber. He had no way of telling whether he was at police headquarters or at some other site reserved for prisoners who "disappeared," but he wasn't concerned about municipal geography.

No matter how you sliced it, he was up Shit Creek.

His captors had refused to notify the U.S. consulate, and they had worked him over in a quasi-public place. Jack had no reason to believe his other rights would be respected now that he was chained and isolated in a holding cell.

They wanted information, obviously, but he dared not speak until he knew which side these cops were on. If they were honest officers who responded overzealously to shootings in the park, he had a chance. If they were bought and paid for by Rodriguez, sent to break his cover, Fowler knew he was as good as dead.

He heard footsteps circling the room behind him, and he kept his head down, lowering his eyelids. Stall them if you can. Delay the pain as long as possible.

Rough fingers tangled in his hair and jerked his head back, straining Fowler's neck. His eyes came open grudgingly to focus on a black, inverted face.

"He's back," the uniform advised a second party, somewhere out of view.

The suit stepped out in front of Fowler, stripped to shirtsleeves now, the vest and slacks immaculate. The garments looked expensive, and Fowler was losing hope as he began to estimate a Nassau homicide detective's salary.

"What brings you to the islands, Mr. Fraser?"

"I'm a businessman."

"What business are you in?"

"Commodities."

The suit was scowling at him with contempt. "You deal in drugs, is that correct?"

"I moved some penicillin once to Trinidad. It's no big deal."

The suit glanced up and nodded, and Fowler braced to take it as the hulking uniform came back and slammed a fist into his unprotected ribs. It took breath to scream, and Fowler did not make a sound.

"I've checked your background in Miami, Mr. Fraser. You are known to the police as a narcotics dealer and a thief. Today in Nassau you have killed four men, a fifth will almost surely die before the night is out."

"That's self-defense. Guys come at me with guns, no cops around to save the day, so I handle it myself."

"Possession of a pistol in the city is a separate felony," the suit replied. "Of course, if there were some extenuating circumstance..."

"Such as?"

"Things are not always what they seem. A name, for instance—or a reputation. If you were a law enforcement officer perhaps, on some assignment beneficial to my government as well as yours... adjustments could be made."

Jack forced a crooked smile. "Let's get this straight. You guys want me to tell you I'm a cop?"

"I want the *truth*. Your name. Your business in the islands. Your intentions toward the sovereign state of Bahama."

Jack knew he had to tough it out.

"I've talked my business over with a friend of yours already. Call up Gorman Poole in Freeport if you want the shopping list. Or better yet, why don't you ask the guy who bought that suit?"

He missed the signal this time, but the uniform was back and swinging, fists like knobby wooden clubs connecting with his abdomen, his face. Warm blood and sweat rained on his chest. The suit called off his muscle sometime later, squatting down so Fowler would not have to raise his head to look him in the eye.

"We shall begin, as you would say, from scratch. Your name?"

BY NIGHTFALL, Prudence Sullivan was worried. She had given up on waiting, tried the Graycliff half a dozen times, but Fraser's telephone rang on and on without relief. The desk clerk seemed deliberately evasive when she asked if there were any messages or if there was a time when Mr. Fraser was expected back.

She recognized the smell of trouble, but she had no inkling what to do. It would be foolish—even dangerous—to visit the hotel herself. At best the trip would be a waste, with Fraser gone; at worst she would reveal herself to anyone maintaining a surveillance of his rooms. So far, the Graycliff's operator only knew that Fraser kept on getting phone calls from a woman, but they did not know her name or where she could be found. She meant to keep it that way if she could.

"What *is* it?"

Startled by the fact that she had spoken to an empty room, she went and poured herself a glass of wine to calm her nerves. There were at least a hundred reasons Fraser might be out tonight. He was out to dinner. Taking in a show. Conducting business with Ornelas. Meeting Weldon Glass.

It never crossed her mind that he was with another woman. Not that they had formed a lasting bond the night before, but Fraser had his hands full with his work. On top of that, he knew she was available and willing, if he wanted sex. With pardonable pride, she told herself he did not *need* another woman here and now.

The flip side of her upbeat possibilities was something else again. Abduction. Death. Arrest. Evacuation from the islands if he thought his cover had been blown.

If Fraser disappeared, what would become of Prudence and the printouts she had taken from the Merchants Bank? Her wisest course of action, in the circumstances, was to destroy the evidence. A simple match would do the job, or she could tear them up and flush them down the toilet and away. Without the papers, no one could establish any working link between herself and the American.

Unless he talked.

A chill ran down her spine as she imagined Fraser undergoing torture, hypodermic needles pumping drugs to loosen his tongue. If she was named, a year or two in prison for her violation of the banking laws would be the least of her concerns. The men who laundered their illicit funds through Merchants Bank would see her dead before she had a chance to speak with the authorities.

She had the papers in her hand, considering the swiftest, surest method of disposal, when she caught herself. It was a grave mistake to let her own imagination run away like this. If Fraser *was* interrogated, and he *did* give up her name, then it would make no difference whether she retained the printouts or destroyed them. On the other hand, if Fraser was alive and well, she had to give him time to get in touch and make the pickup.

Prudence hid the papers underneath a tray of ice cubes in her freezer. For tonight at least she would maintain her vigil, waiting for a call. If Fraser had not taken steps to get in touch with her by quitting time tomorrow, she would have to think again.

But in the meantime, she would sip her wine and wait. Turn on the television, a Miami station, and forget about the danger to herself.

As if she could.

She had been foolish, idiotic, offering assistance and her body to a man she had barely met. The talk about her brother, the comparison with Fraser's murdered friend, had broken down the walls of her resistance in a manner she did not anticipate. Embarrassed by the ease of her surrender, Prudence felt her cheeks flush brilliant crimson. It was bad enough that she had taken him to bed, a perfect stranger, but she had agreed to risk her life as well.

The doorbell startled her, and she spilled a dash of wine across her skirt.

"Goddamn it!"

She moved toward the door reluctantly, knowing it was no use trying to pretend that she was not at home. The caller would have seen her lights and heard the television; if he listened closely, he could probably detect her footsteps in the entry hall.

There was a peephole in the door, and Prudence used it, one eye pressed against the viewing lens. Despite distortion from the fish-eye she immediately recognized the solemn face of Weldon Glass.

"Come in."

She latched the door behind him, glad that he was there and frightened of his presence all at once. Instinctively she knew the call could only mean bad news.

"What is it?"

"Trouble. Have you seen the news?"

She shook her head. "Not yet."

"Ornelas sent his men for Fraser. There was shooting. Men were killed."

"And Fraser?"

"He's in custody," said Glass. "Collect your things. He can't last very long."

JORGE RODRIGUEZ HEARD the telephone ring twice before his houseman picked it up. The dealer never answered calls himself, and at the moment he was occupied with the naked blonde in his bed.

The ceiling of his bedroom captured their reflection, her ivory body slithering sinuously around his darker flesh in the moonlike glow of the mirrors.

He liked the view and pushed her farther down along his torso, reveling in the warm sensations, but now Rodriguez became distracted wondering about the call. It irked him, knowing that his privacy could be invaded, pleasure interrupted anytime a member of his staff required advice.

He shifted slightly on the mattress, thrusting with his hips to give the blonde a challenge. She was equal to the task, responding with an ardor that was either very real or very well rehearsed. Rodriguez had no interest in sincerity, but he demanded proper service from his staff and hired woman alike.

He always got his money's worth.

A knocking on the door disturbed the blonde, and Rodriguez reached down to nudge her. "Nobody said for you to stop." Then he faced the bedroom door and barked, "Come in."

The houseman did not give the blonde a second glance. "It's Nassau, *jefe*."

"Plug me in."

The houseman knelt and put the phone jack in the wall, then lifted the receiver, passed it to Rodriguez and excused himself.

"Jorge?"

The voice of Rafael Ornelas sounded distant, strained. Bad news.

"What is it, Rafael?"

"This Fowler."

"*¿Sí?*"

"I sent some people for him like you said. He's pretty good, this guy."

"He got away."

It did not come out sounding like a question, but Ornelas felt compelled to answer anyway.

"Eight men, I sent. I've got four dead and two more in the hospital."

"The other two?"

"He knocked one of them out. That is, he knocked *two* of them out and shot five more. One of the guys he slugged woke up and got away."

"That still leaves one," Rodriguez said.

"The driver, yeah. He had to split before the cops showed up."

"Where's Fowler now?"

"Thing is, Jorge, our guy in Freeport must've talked to someone. Cops were waiting back at Fraser's room. They've got him."

"*Which* cops?"

"They're on our pad, don't worry. They've got Fowler stashed away somewhere so they can question him."

"You must be getting soft, you let police do all the work."

"Well, hey, I thought—"

"Don't think!" Rodriguez snapped. "I told you to put a lid on Fowler, rub him out. That's what I meant. Not give him to the cops and let them question him about our business. Am I getting through?"

"I hear you *jefe*." The man sounded peevish, like an injured child.

"I hope so, Rafael. You fuck this up, I'll have to find somebody else can do the job."

"It's in the bag."

"So wrap it up. And don't call back until you do it right."

He dropped the telephone receiver in its cradle, trying hard to focus his attention on the blonde. The last few moments of his conversation with Ornelas, he could feel his interest flagging, but she revived it in moments and Rodriguez gave himself to the sensations, drifting, con-

fident that Rafael would find a way to save the game in
Nassau. There was probably no harm in Fowler spilling
what he knew to crooked native cops, but any leak was a
potential danger point. Rodriguez was a firm believer in
the principle of need-to-know, and there were damned
few people in the islands cleared for access to the details
of his operation in Miami. Rafael knew most of it, of
course; the bankers had a list of names and numbers in
their confidential files, but they were not apprised of who
was who in southern Florida. It made no difference to a
hard-core money mover whether his depositors were
dealers, kinky cops or lying politicians, gospel priests or
working whores. The bottom line was cash and all the
pleasures it could buy.

Their scenic encounter in bed was coming to an end as
Rodriguez stiffened in the anticipation of his climax. She
could feel it coming, and even though he was the customer, the one in control, Rodriguez knew it gave her a
sense of primal power to see him in his moment of release. He thrust her away from him, and she left to brush
her teeth and shower, while he lay immobile on the bed.
He saw no need for conversation or endearments in the
wake of sex. It was a simple business deal, a need fulfilled, and he had paid the blonde up front. She would
return tomorrow night if she was summoned, or he might
see fit to call on someone else.

If there was good news from the islands, cause for cel-
ebration, he might even spring for twins.

But in the meantime, he would have to wait. Ornelas
understood his orders and the price of failure. He had
never let Rodriguez down before, and there was no good
reason to anticipate a failure.

If Fowler was in custody, he made a sitting target.
Perfect.

They could think about the cleanup later, mending fences in the wake of violence that would cause embarrassment to the prime minister in Nassau, dealing with the loose ends as they were revealed.

One such was Gorman Poole.

The man had proven useful in his way, but he was filled with self-importance, half believing he was indispensable to the cartel. It was a fatal error, and Rodriguez knew that he would have to shop around for Poole's replacement, and soon.

But first, the Fed.

When he was gone, the climate in Miami would return to normal, Ervin Steele and his surviving officers could do their job, and the remaining independent dealers would be forced to fall in line.

It was inevitable.

Fate was smiling on Jorge Rodriguez, calling him by name.

He was about to gain a stranglehold on cocaine traffic in Miami, and there was no one who could stop him now.

18

The address of the safehouse was an open secret to police in Nassau. Theoretically acquired for the protection of endangered witnesses and snitches, it had served the designated function only once or twice since it was purchased from a covert slush fund registered in non-existent names. It served more often as a holding pen for certain prisoners who needed rough persuasion to cooperate with an investigation in progress. Some of them had subsequently disappeared.

In short, the Nassau safehouse was not safe.

A simple phone call was enough for Weldon Glass to know that Fraser had not been confined in ordinary quarters at the jail. Another, to a friend in the detective bureau, had confirmed his placement at the safehouse, where a special team was working overtime to find out what he knew about the shootings at Fort Montagu.

And if he broke, there would be hell to pay.

The secret of successful penetration, Glass decided, was audacity. He would be facing odds of three or four to one at least, and he would have to get inside the house before he even had a chance of helping Fraser out. The best approach was a direct approach, regardless of the risk.

He drove by, counting cars—two dark sedans, the standard unmarked vehicle—then parked against the curb in front. The standard-issue sidearm for police in Nassau was a .38 revolver, either Colt or Smith & Wesson, but for this job Glass had backed his two-inch snubby up with an impressive U.S. Army .45. Before he left the car, unlocked for hasty getaways, he double-checked the automatic to be sure it had a live round in the chamber, thumbing back the hammer so that it was cocked and locked before he tucked it in his waistband underneath the flowered shirt.

Glass palmed his shield as he approached the door, prepared for anything as he reached out and pressed the bell. He heard the chimes inside, abrupt, off-key, as if they knew his visit meant bad news. He was about to try again when he detected heavy footsteps just beyond the door.

A two-by-three-inch peephole opened to reveal one eye, some chocolate skin, a portion of a nose.

"Whozat?"

Glass held his shield up to the peephole, striving for a measure of sincerity as he announced, "Headquarters sent me down to help you out."

"We don't need any help," the baleful eye replied.

"You want me to tell that to the chief, okay. Just let me have your number so he doesn't mix you up with any-body else."

"Hold on."

The peephole closed, and Weldon heard at least three different locks released, together with a chain, before the door swung open to admit him. On the other side, an of-ficer in uniform stood glaring at him, taller by at least six inches, heavier by eighty pounds or more.

"I'd better see that badge again."

Glass let him see the .45 instead, its muzzle looking huge on the receiving end.

"One sound and you're a memory."

The uniform responded with a sneer, but kept his mouth shut, making no attempt to rush the gun or draw his own.

"Your prisoner," said Glass. "Where is he?"

"In the basement."

"Stairs?"

"The kitchen pantry."

Weldon looked for twitches that would indicate deception and found none. "How many with him?"

"One detective, one patrolman."

"Turn around and face the wall."

He did as he was told, instinctively assuming the position for a frisk. Instead of going for his weapon first, Glass stepped in close and cracked the muzzle of his .45 across the tall man's skull. His forehead met the wall, a solid thump, but he was still not out of it, and Weldon had to slug him one more time to make it stick.

Glass knelt beside the prostrate figure, working fast in case the men downstairs were tempted to investigate the unexpected noise. He drew the big man's hands behind his back and used the handcuffs from his belt to keep them there. A pocket of the blue serge slacks gave up a handkerchief, and Weldon stuffed it into the patrolman's mouth. He also took the big man's gun, a Smith & Wesson .38, before he rose and went to find the basement stairs.

One down and two to go.

It would be ugly if he had to use the guns, but Glass had come too far to turn back now. He was committed and he had to follow through, regardless of the cost.

He found the pantry easily—the house was not that large—and opened up a closet by mistake before he found the hidden stairs. He paused and listened at the door, picking up some muffled sounds that he could not identify.

No time to waste.

He opened up the door and started down the stairs, a gun in each hand.

"LET'S TRY AGAIN."

The black detective's face was out of focus, blurry, even though he seemed to be within arm's reach. Jack Fowler shook his head to clear the image, instantly regretting it as jolts of pain shot through his skull. His ribs and stomach throbbed in counterpoint, the combined effect producing an erratic symphony of suffering.

"You are an agent of the U.S. government, correct?"

"I answered that already," Fowler said, finding the act of speaking painful in itself.

The black face smiled without a hint of mirth.

"Persistence is a virtue, Mr. Fowler, but it also has a price. Your lies are not convincing in the face of so much independent evidence."

A simple shrug left Fowler feeling drained. "You know the answers going in, seems like a waste of time to ask the questions."

Straightening and stepping back, the suit glanced over Fowler's shoulder, toward the waiting uniform. "Continue."

Fowler braced himself as best he could, unable to anticipate the angle of attack. He barely registered the sound of footsteps on a flight of wooden stairs somewhere behind him, muted by the echo of a gunshot in the claustrophobic room.

"Enough!"

He knew the voice should be familiar, but his mind would not give up a name.

The black detective had his hands raised, glaring at the new arrival and his gun. He wore a snub-nosed pistol on his hip but made no move to reach it as discretion won over valor in a pinch.

"You're making a mistake," he said.

"Perhaps, but you should humor me. Go stand against the wall."

The uniform passed Fowler on his left, perhaps ten feet from the detective. He was halfway to the wall before he made his move, a clumsy spin and a not so quick draw borrowed from a 1960s Western movie, squeezing off a hasty, wasted round from his revolver as he turned.

The new arrival shot him twice—a different, larger gun—and Fowler saw the big man lifted off his feet, propelled against the wall. He flattened up against the bricks with the resilience of a beanbag, glassy eyes locked open, sightless, as he slithered to the floor.

If the detective had an urge to join him, it was instantly discarded. Moving with exaggerated care, he turned and placed his palms against the cinder blocks, feet spread a yard or so apart. And Fowler recognized the man who stepped in close behind the detective to club him behind the ear with what appeared to be a GI .45.

The one-man rescue team was Weldon Glass.

He spent a moment stripping weapons from the prostrate bodies, sliding them across the floor and out of reach, before he palmed a handcuff key and doubled back to Fowler's chair.

"You're fit to travel?"

"Have I got an option?"

"No."

Jack found his clothing underneath the stairs, together with his shoulder holster and the Glock. Glass spent a moment putting cuffs on the detective, with Fowler getting dressed as swiftly as he could and replenishing the reclaimed automatic's magazine.

"I have a speedboat waiting," Glass informed him. "You can trust the pilot with your life. He will deliver you to Morgan's Bluff on Andros Island where a flight has been arranged."

"I need to get in touch with Prudence first."

"She's waiting at the dock," said Glass, "and we are running out of time. My car's outside."

Upstairs they passed another snoozing uniform, hands cuffed behind his back. Glass closed the door behind them, automatic locks engaged, and struck off down the walkway toward his baby-blue Mercedes waiting at the curb.

At least I'm running out in style, thought Fowler, following along with every muscle in his body throbbing out a different kind of pain. He could have easily surrendered to his weakness, stretched out on the grass to sleep, but Glass was right.

There was no visible alternative to flight.

They reached the car, and Glass slid in behind the wheel. Jack lagged a pace or two behind, but he was opening the rider's door when headlights pinned him, fast approaching from the far end of the block. He froze, ignoring Weldon's call to hurry, praying that the car belonged to local residents, its turning up just now a mere coincidence. His hopes were shattered as the unknown driver slowed for just a moment, taking stock of what he saw, and then accelerated toward the parked Mercedes with an angry screech of rubber.

"Will you hurry, damn it?"

Weldon had the luxury sedan in gear as Fowler slammed his door, already groping for the automatic in his shoulder rig. Glass stood on the accelerator, steering with his left hand while his right slid out the open driver's window, wrapped around the big Colt .45.

"Hold on!" he snapped, but rushing wind and sudden gunfire whipped his words away.

IN OTHER CIRCUMSTANCES, Rafael Ornelas would have let the hit team do its job alone while he stayed home and waited for reports, but he could not afford to take the casual approach tonight. Already chastised by Rodriguez for initial failure, he was looking at disaster—worse—if he let Fowler slip the net a second time. On top of that, his soldiers would be dealing with police, and they did not possess the requisite finesse for handling negotiations in the proper style.

He would succeed tonight because he had to. Failure was completely unacceptable, the kiss of death.

Ornelas rode the shotgun seat beside the driver; three men were seated in the back with automatic weapons, just in case. He carried seven thousand dollars and a sleek Beretta automatic pistol on his person, equally prepared to grease the officer or to take their prisoner by force, depending on the situation he discovered when they reached their destination.

It had cost him nothing to discover where the prisoner was being held. A desk clerk at the station house was on retainer with the syndicate, and he supplied directions to the safehouse free of charge, without a second thought. A twenty-minute drive across the causeway, onto Potter's Cay and south on Mackey Street, then half a dozen turns put them on the avenue they sought.

"*¿Quién es?*"

The wheelman hesitated, braking as he made the final turn, his headlights framing a Mercedes at the curb downrange. Ornelas glimpsed a black man in a flowered shirt just climbing in behind the wheel, an Anglo on the sidewalk turning toward their lights and giving Rafael a perfect chance to see his face.

"That's Fowler! Take him!"

Rafael was digging for his pistol as their driver hit the gas, and the acceleration pressed him against his seat. He fumbled the Beretta clear, the wind roaring as he cranked his window down. Behind him one of his torpedos was already firing from the driver's side, the muzzle-flashes from his Uzi cutting through the night like summer lightning.

The BMW's right-hand drive prevented Rafael from firing as they passed the first time, but he was conscious of the other wheelman shooting back, his rounds impacting on the body of their car like hammer blows. At least one bullet found the torpedo on the driver's side and punched him backward in his seat, blood spouting from his neck, his Uzi lost outside the car.

Their driver cursed, then hit the brakes, half skidding through a U-turn in the middle of the street. He nearly stalled the engine, saved it at the final instant and took off in hot pursuit of the Mercedes, slowly gaining ground. Behind Ornelas, the surviving gunners shoved their comrade to the floor, one sliding over in a pool of blood to take the right-hand window, while the other took the left.

Ahead of them, the Mercedes was weaving back and forth to keep the BMW from overtaking for a killing shot. Ornelas shoved his pistol out the window and fired twice without effect, but it felt good to shoot in any case. The back-seat gunners limited themselves to measured bursts, first one and then the other, firing only when the blue Mercedes veered across respective lines of sight.

Three blocks and they had scored a dozen or more hits without their target slowing down, when suddenly the blue sedan drifted to the right and stayed there, giving them a chance to close up on the rider's side.

"Come on!" Ornelas shouted at his driver. *"¡Vamos!"*

"But *jefe*—"

"Go!"

The BMW hurtled forward, gaining on the left-hand side of the Mercedes, cutting off one back-seat gunner's field of fire. The other emptied one magazine and fumbled for another, hastily reloading as they pulled abreast of their intended prey.

Ornelas was surprised to see an empty seat beside the other driver... or was Fowler merely hiding underneath the dash? He got his answer when a battered face appeared *behind* the shotgun seat, an automatic pistol stretching out to bridge the gap between their vehicles. Momentum whipped the sound of shots away, but he could see the muzzle-flashes, heard the smack of bullets striking flesh before his driver slumped across the steering wheel.

Ornelas tasted blood and wondered if it was his own, but he would have no time to contemplate the problem. Driverless, the BMW veered hard left and rammed a stationary panel truck against the curb. The windshield rushed to meet Ornelas, and there was not even time to scream.

THE SPEEDBOAT WAS a low-slung cigarette, its pilot black and young. Before Glass parked the car, Fowler caught a glimpse of Prudence pacing up and down the dock at Prince George Wharf, arms crossed below her breasts, her face a study in anxiety.

"You're coming?"

"No," Glass said, "I still have work to do in Nassau."

"With a dead cop on your hands?"

"Before they charge me, someone must explain what they were doing at the safehouse with a prisoner no one is willing to identify. If there are charges filed, I won't go down alone."

"Still safer in the States," said Fowler. "I could pull some strings, throw in a reference from Teddy Jakes."

"You're wasting time," the black man told him. "Go."

He went, the dome light showing Fowler that the front of Weldon's shirt was drenched in blood, dark splotches soaking through his baggy slacks.

"For Christ's sake—"

"Go!"

As Weldon spoke, he put the car in gear and started rolling, the momentum slamming Fowler's door before he traveled half a block. The car was weaving slightly, but he made the intersection, took a left and disappeared from view.

"My God, what happened to your face?"

He forced a smile for Prudence, holding her at arm's length when she tried for an embrace. "The same thing as my ribs," he said. "A little disagreement with the local heat."

"Are you all right?"

"I'll be a damn sight better once we're on that plane. You got the paperwork?"

"Right here." She clutched a giant purse, but the rest of her luggage—what little there was of it—was waiting in the boat.

"They didn't give me time to pack," said Fowler, "so I guess we're set."

"What happens now?" she asked.

"We run like hell until we hit Miami. Once we're there, I finish what I started with Rodriguez."

"And for me?"

"Some testimony when we get that far. Beyond the trial, you're free and clear. The federal witness program offers relocation, or I'll help you on my own if you prefer."

This time she managed to produce a smile. "I think I like that better, Jason."

"Jack."

The lady looked confused.

"I'll fill you in before we hit Miami," Fowler said. "The high points, anyway. Who knows, it may be just like starting out from scratch."

19

The strike team had assembled in a basement chamber of the Federal Building in Miami, waiting for the word. A mixed bag drawn from several agencies, the force included six men from the DEA, a four-man SWAT contingent from the FBI, three men from ATF to check for federal firearms violations, and a dozen U.S. Marshals called from home to fill the ranks. Each man had come equipped with Kevlar vest and gas mask, standard sidearms and another weapon of his choice—including riot shotguns, M-16s, high-powered hunting rifles, several compact submachine guns. Conversation died as Rudy Stano took the podium.

"Okay," he said, "let's get this sideshow on the road. Most of you don't know why you're here, and that's deliberate. No slap at any person or department in particular, but we've had problems out the ass with leaks on this one. I'm the plumber."

Scattered chuckles came from the audience, but Fowler noticed others frowning to themselves. They all had personal experience with information leaks inside their separate agencies, but none of them enjoyed becoming targets of suspicion in themselves.

"From this point on," said Stano, "we'll be operating under maximum security. Aside from regional directors or agents in charge of your several departments, no one else outside this room knows where we're going, what we mean to do."

"Hell, even *we* don't know."

The comment emanated from the FBI contingent, and it brought a crooked grin to Stano's face. "Good point. Somebody want to kill the lights?"

A nervous hush descended as the lights dimmed, then Stano keyed a button on the podium to activate a slide projector mounted on a rolling stand beside him. Suddenly a giant face filled up the bare white wall to Stano's right.

"Jorge Luis Rodriguez. If you watch TV or read the papers, you should recognize the name. He moved enough cocaine through southern Florida last year to satisfy at least one-fourth of the users nationwide. These days he's working on a localized monopoly, including the reported use of Metro-Dade patrolmen to eliminate his competition on the street. In case you're wondering, that's why you don't see any local uniforms included in our little gathering. We frankly don't know who to trust."

There was some murmuring at that, and Stano let it run its course before continuing.

"I don't like end runs any more than you do," he went on, when it was quiet. "If there's one thing we don't need, it's more bad feeling in the ranks. But we've uncovered evidence that sets Rodriguez up for federal prosecution, major asset seizures, a potential deathblow to his operation in Miami. It's been too expensive for a bluesuit on the pad to scrub our action when we're sitting on the one-yard line."

The picture on the wall behind him changed to a bird's-eye view of wooded grounds and buildings, cars and human figures shrunken down to matchbox size.

"You're looking at the target, an aerial of the Rodriguez spread in Coral Gables, near the Riviera Golf Course. That's a dock you see on the canal, the lower right-hand corner, with a speedboat sitting there. It's his escape hatch, two miles down to Biscayne Bay and open water if we give him half a chance. I need a couple volunteers who don't get seasick for the backdoor detail, cut him off in case he tries to run.''

"You've got it," said a member of the U.S. Marshal's team, a burly black man with an Uzi submachine gun in his lap.

"Okay, that's fine. We've got a cigarette on standby at the mouth of the canal. It goes that way, you're cleared to ram him, blow him up, whatever. Just remember what What's-his-name said: 'They shall not pass.'''

The marshal said, "I'm thinking that was General Patton."

"Guess again," one of the G-men countered. "Sounds more like my daughter's English teacher."

"Okay, let's wrap this up," said Stano, turning to the aerial display and pointing with a yardstick. "They have people on the gate right here, and others work the grounds. No evidence of any dogs that we could see, but count on heavy hardware. Whether they resist or fold depends on how *El Jefe*'s feeling at the moment."

"If they fight?"

"No contest. You protect yourselves and one another. We've got lawful warrants going in. Somebody wants to shoot it out, make sure you win."

"How many hardguys on the grounds, you figure?"

"That's unknown. I'd be surprised if there were less than eight or ten guys around at any given time."

"Okay."

"I'm leading four men to the gate in front," said Stano. "If they let us in without a beef, that's cool. If not, at least we'll keep them occupied awhile. Jack Fowler will be taking seven with him in a chopper, setting down inside the compound near the house. With two men watching the canal, that leaves two five-man teams to mop up the perimeter on north and south. You'll have to climb an eight-foot wall, but we've got ladders waiting for you. Any questions?''

There were several, and he dealt with each in turn, and Jack Fowler tuned out and concentrated on his job. They had to bag Rodriguez first, before they moved against Lieutenant Ervin Steele, because they did not know his cronies on the force, and any leak about a crackdown would allow Rodriguez time to slip away.

He thought of Weldon Glass and felt a sour churning in his stomach. Fowler's calls to Nassau had elicited no useful information on the wounded officer's condition. His superiors were playing dumb, and Teddy Jakes had so far come up empty when he asked around.

But it was payback time. Jack Fowler felt it in his gut. And he could hardly wait.

JORGE RODRIGUEZ passed on the Ornelas funeral service. Rafael was stupid. *Anyone* who let himself get killed that way was stupid, when you thought about it. Down in Nassau they were holding all the cards, and still he couldn't win the fucking game.

Bone stupid, right.

The worst part was that Fowler had escaped again. Ornelas and his men had bagged a local cop, but that was little consolation with the Fed still at large. Considering adverse publicity, the murder of another cop made matters worse, with Fowler safe and sound.

Rodriguez did not even know the bastard, and he wanted Fowler dead. *Needed* him dead, the way some people need their alcohol or drugs to make it through the day. He had become obsessed with rubbing Fowler out, and now that Rafael had blown it in the islands, it was reasonable to assume the Fed would make his way back to Miami.

There was something else, some woman missing from the Merchants Bank in Nassau, but Rodriguez didn't know exactly what to make of it so far. According to the first reports, no valuables or records were reported missing, and for all he knew the bitch might be shacked up somewhere or lying in the Nassau morgue, the victim of a hit-and-run. In other circumstances, he wouldn't have given it a second thought, but the coincidence set his teeth on edge.

Jack Fowler had to be dealt with first, but he could not afford to do the job himself. There had been too much heat around to settle Fowler's hash. At least the death of one patrolman had diverted some of the attention to another quarter, but Rodriguez knew that it would all come back to him if they looked long and hard enough.

No, Rodriguez did not plan to do the job personally, but it would have been a kick to question Fowler, make him squirm and scream for several days before they put a mercy bullet through the fucker's head. Or maybe set his ass on fire and watch him fry, the way they used to do just for fun with homeless bums in Medellín.

You had to take your jollies where you found them in the coca trade.

And this time, of necessity, Rodriguez had to delegate responsibility for Fowler's execution to an independent hitter, someone who could do the job without establishing a trail of evidence to the Colombian cartel.

Someone like Ervin Steele from Metro-Dade.

The cops had screwed up twice, and they were under scrutiny from members of their own department, but they had a stake in seeing Fowler put away while the surviving members of the hit team still had jobs to save.

Rodriguez made the call himself, not trusting it to anybody else. Steele might have tried to argue with his second in command, come up with some excuse that everybody knew was bullshit, but he would follow orders from the man who held the strings. The telephone rang half a dozen times before a gruff, familiar voice came on the line.

"Narcotics, Steele."

"We need to talk."

The narc lieutenant hesitated, and Rodriguez pictured the expression on his face, a furtive glance beyond his door to see if anyone was loitering around to eavesdrop.

"When?"

"Right now."

"That's hard. I've got a shitload of reports to read and—"

"Now," Rodriguez snapped. "Make time."

"Okay, no problem. Did you have a place in mind?"

"I'm staying home tonight."

"You think that's wise?"

He was concerned about surveillance, but Rodriguez didn't care. "You're talking to a suspect, right? It wouldn't be the first time you went to someone's home."

"I guess."

"You're on the clock. Don't keep me waiting."

Dropping the receiver in its cradle, he allowed himself a smile. The exercise of power always left him feeling stronger, like a bodybuilder after working out. Rodriguez loved to make men bow and scrape, surrendering their dignity upon demand. It made him special, someone to be reckoned with.

Despite his note of urgency, Rodriguez knew it would require some time for Steele to reach his house. There were procedures to be followed by an officer on duty when he left the station house; he had to fabricate a destination where he could be reached in case of an emergency, devise some explanation in advance for phone calls that would not go through. Rodriguez trusted Ervin Steele to hide his tracks with care. If nothing else, the narc lieutenant was a streetwise operator, reasonably skilled at covering his ass.

That skill would come in handy on the Fowler contract, with the heat already focused on Narcotics after Keegan's death and two attacks upon the Fed. If Steele's subordinates were too incompetent to do the job, he might be forced to handle it alone.

Tough shit.

The guy was being paid enough to take some risks along the way, and there were always choices. Do or die, damn right.

If Steele had trouble making up his mind, Rodriguez would be glad to help him, maybe flip a coin to see if he would do his job or bite the bullet. Either way, it would mean one less problem underfoot.

Look at it that way, and Rodriguez couldn't lose.

The dealer poured himself a drink and settled back to wait.

"IF HE THINKS I'm going out there by myself, the bastard needs to have his head examined."

"So," Detective Richard Skirvin answered, "what's the game?"

"A show of force," Steele said. "You back me up, so Rodriguez knows he can't be pushing us around."

"The three of us? What's that, compared to all the men he's got?"

The question came from Sergeant Frank Meadows, Steele's immediate subordinate in Metro-Dade Narcotics.

"Not three *guys*," Steele told him, quickly running out of patience. "Three *policemen*. He's got heat enough from Hicks and Keegan as it is."

"We've all got heat from Hicks and Keegan," Meadows said.

"My point is that Rodriguez can't afford to waste three cops. One guy, he might be tempted, but he isn't dumb enough to think that he would get away with three. No way."

"You want to muscle him or what?" asked Skirvin.

"All I'm gonna do is listen to the man, okay? He didn't spell out exactly what he wants, but I don't need a psychic flash to dope it out. They made a run at Fowler in the islands, and they fucked it up. Smart money says he's back in town by now, and our Colombian *compadre*'s getting nervous."

"First he doesn't want us hitting Fowler," Skirvin muttered, "but now he does. The fucker can't make up his mind."

"One thing for sure," said Steele. "We'll have to renegotiate the going price."

"Damn straight."

"He won't be happy," Meadows said.

"Somebody ask me if I care."

Dick Skirvin grinned. "You care, Lieutenant?"

"Fuck, no."

"I never counted on a war against Rodriguez," Meadows grumbled.

"It'll never come to that. Hell, I don't mean to hold the bastard up, but fair is fair. The price for rousting dealers doesn't cover wasting Feds, that's all."

"He'll shit a brick."

"So bring some ass-wipes with you. While you're at it, better bring some extra hardware . . . just in case."

"I knew it."

"Nothing heavy," Steele replied. "These macho types respect a man who deals from strength. We go in looking weak, he's bound to try and walk all over us. We have to flex a little muscle—it just shows him we mean business.''

"I don't like it,'' Meadows said.

Steele pinned him with an icy glare, not moving toward his gun since they were sitting in his office with six or seven other dicks outside the wall of pebbled glass just ten feet away.

"So, are you in or out?'' he asked.

"You ask that like I've got a choice.''

"We've all got choices, Frank.''

There could be no mistake about his tone, the meaning of his words. Frank Meadows spent a moment thinking of replies that he could use, discarding each in turn.

"Okay, I'm in.''

"That's fine. Suit up and meet me down in the garage, ten minutes. You keep a guy like Jorge waiting, he gets nervous.''

All alone, Steele checked his Bren Ten automatic's load, returned it to his shoulder holster. He was not expecting any overt violence from Rodriguez, but it never hurt to be prepared. The Boy Scouts taught him that when he was ten years old, and everything he knew about the real world had confirmed that simple rule.

Preparedness could save your ass in killing situations, when a man who put his trust in luck went down the tubes. Steele made his own luck going in. He put his trust where it belonged—in number one.

Rodriguez was a predator, his senses finely tuned to pick out fear and weakness in prospective victims. Dealing with a predator, the first thing that you learned was never turn your back, and never run away.

Steele meant to stand his ground and make a profit in the bargain.

He might even make a killing.

You could never tell.

20

The helicopter was a Bell UH-1D, the famous "Huey" used so frequently in Vietnam for medical evacuations and insertion of assault teams into hostile landing zones. Jack Fowler did not care for the analogy, all things considered, but it seemed to fit. There was a real potential for some nasty action on the ground at the Rodriguez compound, and he was not thrilled about the odds.

His flying squad consisted of three Drug Enforcement agents and the four-man Bureau SWAT team, all in black, with their respective agencies identified across their backs in foot-high Day-Glo letters. They were loaded up for bear with shotguns, submachine guns, automatic rifles, sidearms—and he still had doubts about the plan.

It wasn't by any means inconceivable that Rodriguez had fifty-caliber machine guns hidden in the undergrowth around his house, troops armed with frag grenades and rockets hiding in the house. The Franchi LAW semiautomatic 12-gauge shotgun braced across his lap seemed suddenly inadequate, compared to what they might be facing when they hit the ground.

Jack told himself they were prepared for anything, their odds improved by Rudy Stano's planned diversion at the gate. If there was trouble, it would start right there with Rudy, one more Drug Enforcement agent and three members of the IRS Alcohol, Tobacco and Firearms unit facing down armed guards behind an eight-foot wrought iron barrier. The Huey was supposed to make its drop some ninety seconds after Stano reached the gate, and well before the teams of U.S. Marshals started scaling walls on the perimeter.

No sweat, unless their estimates of the defense came in low and they were suddenly outnumbered two or three to one. A heavy hitter like Rodriguez, you could never tell when paranoia might persuade him that a couple dozen bodyguards were needed on a given night.

Jack pictured Custer at the Little Big Horn, only this time he was being overrun by hundreds of Colombian guerillas armed with M-16s and Uzis, everybody hosing down the Seventh Cavalry with automatic fire. He pushed the image out of mind and concentrated on the bright lights of Miami, merging into Coral Gables now without an obvious dividing line.

Not long to wait.

Beside him on a metal bench that numbed his ass, Mike Franco of the DEA was checking out the safety on his CAR-15, the shorter, lighter carbine version of the classic M-16. On Franco's right, two other Drug Enforcement agents, Riley and Yamato were attempting to conduct a normal conversation, getting nowhere with the chopper's engine noise.

Directly opposite, his four men from the FBI sat stone-faced, weapons braced between their knees in textbook style. One guy on either side was examining the lights below, their comrades in the middle staring back at Fowler with unreadable expressions, neither hostile nor amused. They clearly knew their jobs, but Fowler had to ask himself if they were really *there*.

How long to reach their destination? They had given Stano and his team a quarter hour's leeway, since the spearhead would be traveling by car. Departure had been carefully coordinated with an eye toward distance, speed and the projected traffic. Stano was in radio communication with the pilot, just in case they hit a snag along the way and needed extra time.

No sweat.

But Fowler's palms were clammy all the same. A storm of contradictory emotions raged inside him: eagerness to see Jorge Rodriguez wearing handcuffs, scowling on his way to jail; a warrior's common fear of facing sudden death and the unknown; regret that he had not been able to arrest Glen Keegan's killers first, before they staged the raid.

As Rudy Stano had explained—and Fowler had reluctantly agreed—it would have been a major goof to drop the net on Ervin Steele before they had Rodriguez in the bag. Despite one kinky narc on ice, they still had no ID on Steele's companions in the drug-extortion ring, and taking down a cop—much less a Metro-Dade lieutenant in Narcotics—would certainly alert Rodriguez to a sweep in progress, giving him a chance to slip away. Conversely, if they bagged the dealer first, there was an outside chance he might roll over on his bluesuit triggermen to cut himself some slack.

And if he didn't, they were left with Steele, indictable on income tax evasion and a list of other federal charges. He could kiss the job goodbye, his pension, everything. The Merchants Bank connection with Rodriguez was enough to earn him prison time instead of mere probation, and he might decide to point a finger in his own self-interest, as they came down to the wire.

It ate at Fowler's gut to think Glen Keegan's killers might be still at large this time tomorrow. Hell, this time next year for all he knew. The one thing putting on a badge had taught him, other than the sheer fragility of human life, was that the good guys didn't always win.

Some days he did not even have a clue who the good guys were.

But he could spot the bad guys coming from a mile away.

"We're getting there," the pilot told them, his voice through his helmet microphone sounding like the automated teller at a drive-through bank.

Jack's stomach told him they were rapidly descending, and he verified it with a quick glance out the open loading bay. The lights down there were getting closer, but he spotted darkness, too. Backyards. Deserted parks and golf links. The canal, where U.S. Marshals would be waiting for Rodriguez if he tried to slip away by boat.

His people knew their moves, and there was nothing more to say.

Jack closed his eyes and concentrated on remembering a childhood prayer. If only he could get it right, before his time ran out....

THE GATE MAN LOOKED confused when Ervin Steele rolled down the driver's window of his El Dorado, checking out Frank Meadows in the shotgun seat, Dick Skirvin in the back. It seemed to Steele the man was counting on his fingers, working on a problem that he could not pass.

"I thought you was supposed to be alone."

"That's your mistake," Steele told him, putting on an ice-cold grin.

"Nobody mentioned anything about these guys."

"What say we all go home? Your boss gets curious, just tell him I was here on time, some fuckhead wouldn't let me in. It's cool."

He had the Caddy in reverse before the gate man stopped him. "Wait a second. I just got to check it out."

Another guy was waiting for him at the gate, and this one had a walkie-talkie. He figured several more they couldn't see, with weapons leveled at the car, but Steele was cool. He watched the joker with the radio say something, rapid-fire, then wait for a response. They argued back and forth a minute, then the gate man doubled back, a sour expression on his face.

"Hokay, you clear. Somebody have to check you at the house."

"Whatever."

There were spotters here and there along the curving drive, most of them packing riot guns or rifles as they made their rounds. Steele parked around in back, the way he always did, and pocketed his keys.

A pair of scowling bookends met them on the lawn, one of them gesturing with meaty hands that he expected them to raise their arms, preliminary to a frisk.

"Get real. We're cops, for Christ's sake. If you think I'm giving up my piece, you're fucking nuts."

The bookends glared some more, nobody moving for a while, but finally they got an escort to the house. More wasted time, as the shooters talked to their foreman, telling him in Spanish that the crazy gringos would not play along and leave their guns behind.

"We're friends here," said the houseman, his expression telling Steele he would rather have had a hungry cannibal drop by for lunch. "This way."

He led them toward the room Rodriguez called his study, telling Skirvin and the sergeant they would have to wait outside while Steele went in to see the man.

"No problem," Meadows told him, flicking on and off a plastic smile. Arms crossed, his fingers were within a few short centimeters of the Ingram submachine gun slung beneath his coat.

"I'm cool," said Skirvin, shifting so the angle of his body took some weight off the 12-gauge stakeout pump wedged underneath his arm.

Rodriguez had his back to Steele, face toward the windows, and he did not turn around at once when the lieutenant entered. "You have heard the news from Nassau?"

"Bits and pieces," Steele replied. "I heard Ornelas bought it. Fowler didn't."

"So. There is a situation we must remedy."

"Who's *we?* Last time I tried to take him out, you damn near bit my head off."

"A mistake, perhaps, although your methods were...untidy."

"Like, you really cleaned things up in Nassau, I suppose."

"We have a common interest, *sí?* It serves us both if Fowler is disposed of quietly. Perhaps, if he should disappear..."

"It won't be easy," Steele replied. "I've got Internal Affairs breathing down my neck, bugging my goddamn phones for all I know. They didn't follow me tonight, but it'll come to that, if something doesn't break."

"You had a plan for some diversionary measure?"

"It's in place," he said. "I put word out that Hicks and Keegan were a team, involved with drugs some way. It takes a while for IAD to run the loose ends down is all. They have to satisfy themselves there's no more cops involved. The trouble is, they see dirt everywhere."

"And Fowler?"

"It's a different thing. If I can find out where he lives—"

A knocking interrupted Steele, the houseman barging in without an invitation, saying something to Rodriguez, and the dealer's face went hard as agate.

"I believe you said you were not followed?"

"Right. So what?"

"I have a team of federal agents at my gate with warrants."

Steele was thinking fast, his stomach knotting as the houseman got his orders and retreated. Suddenly, a too-familiar sound came from outside, the *chop-chop-chop* of rotor blades that readily identified a helicopter setting down.

He saw Rodriguez moving toward the windows, jerking back as someone fired a shot outside and everybody started shooting in a goddamned free-for-all. The dealer made a beeline for his desk and reached inside the upper right-hand drawer, a pistol in his hand when it emerged.

"I cannot tolerate mistakes," Rodriguez told him. "You have failed me once too often, Steele."

But the lieutenant was there ahead of him, his Bren Ten steady in a firm two-handed grip when Jorge turned around. The first round was a heart shot, all he really needed, but he fired once more and struck Rodriguez in the face before his target sprawled behind the desk.

Outside the study, angry voices shouted, followed by a burst of automatic fire. The Ingram? Skirvin's sawed-off shotgun boomed twice before the opposition gave it up. Steele found them waiting for him when he stepped across the threshold to see dead men littering the hall.

"Rodriguez?" Meadows asked, frowning.

"Gone, but not forgotten. We've got Feds outside."

"Well, shit."

"I'd say it's time to split."

"You read my mind."

Their nearest point of exit was the sunken living room, with sliding windows facing on the patio and pool. From there it was a brisk ten-second hike to where the El Dorado waited.

Could they drive away with Feds outside the gate? Steele didn't know for sure, but he was positive that standing still would be a critical mistake. In motion there was hope.

He kept his fingers crossed and got out of there.

JACK FOWLER HAD A GLIMPSE of Stano's people at the gate before the Huey banked and circled toward the mansion, leveling in time to make a fairly painless touchdown on the lawn. He hit the turf, remembering to crouch below the whipping rotor blades, and felt the others piling out behind him, scattering to left and right.

Somebody started firing at them from the house, a tall man with a submachine gun, captured in the glare of floodlights mounted on the eaves. One of the Bureau gunners took him down, a 3-round burst from fifty feet and no mistakes.

The SWAT boys were assigned to cover the Rodriguez hacienda from the front, while Fowler and his three companions made an end run, cutting off escape in back. They ran a deadly zigzag gauntlet, muzzle-flashes winking in the darkness, bullets slicing through the air around them, spurting tufts of grass and sod.

The burst of automatic fire from the direction of the gate was like an echo, barely audible, but even on the run Fowler took it in and wished his best to Rudy. In front of him, a crouching gunner suddenly erupted from the shrubbery, brandishing an M-16, and Fowler hit him with a charge of shot that swept him off his feet.

Two down. How many left to go?

They came around a corner toward the patio and swimming pool in time to meet three men emerging from the house. Both sides stopped short, and Fowler recognized Lieutenant Ervin Steele before the spell was broken, one of Steele's companions grinning as he cut loose with a submachine gun, firing from the hip.

Yamato stopped a couple of the bullets with his Kevlar vest and sat down hard, his automatic rifle ripping off a burst of reflex action. Fowler fired a hasty shot at Steele and winged his short companion, spinning him around as Franco shot him twice more in the back. Then everyone was scattering, the Ingram spitting crazy-eights and keeping Fowler's people on the move until the magazine ran dry.

By that time Steele was a retreating shadow, his companion making tracks and grappling with the Ingram's stubborn magazine. A burst from Riley's carbine knocked him sprawling, ending faceup on the grass.

"The house!" snapped Fowler, pointing toward the open doors and living room beyond. "We have to find Rodriguez."

Franco led the charge, and Fowler left them to it, racing after Steele with murder in his heart. Another corner and he saw the rogue cop climbing into a Cadillac, already turning the ignition key.

Fowler fired: it was a miss.

Still running, he snapped off a shot again, and the pellets from his second charge made pockmarks on the open driver's door. Steele turned the engine over, gunned it, leaning out and firing with a piece that sounded different somehow. Louder by a fraction, like a damned 10-mm, right.

The headlights glaring at him, Fowler stood firm and squeezed off his last six rounds as fast as he could pull the trigger, riding out the recoil as the Caddy's windshield misted over, finally imploding with a crash. The bolt locked open on an empty chamber, and he threw himself aside, the El Dorado roaring past him with a headless driver wedged behind the wheel.

He sat up on the grass and watched it go, the taillights winking out of sight around the corner, Steele's dead weight on the accelerator giving it the impetus to roll until it met some solid obstacle.

More scattered firing sounded from the woods on Fowler's left as the U.S. Marshals moved in from the perimeter and swept everyone before them as they came. Jack spent a moment with his weapon, carefully replenishing the empty magazine and thumbing a live round in the firing chamber as he rose.

And as he headed for the house, Fowler knew the worst of it was over.

EPILOGUE

"Lieutenant Steele killed Glen?"

He recognized the sound of angry disbelief in Molly's voice and nodded solemnly. "Rodriguez, too. The bullets match his piece. There's no mistake."

"The others?"

"Meadows didn't make it. Skirvin's hanging on, and he's been talking more or less nonstop to try and save himself. Fat chance."

"I hope he fries." There was a fury in her eyes that Fowler had not seen before.

"I doubt that anyone can tie him in with Glen," he said. "The dicks at Homicide are checking out ballistics on some other unsolved shootings, going back a year or so, but it's a fishing expedition."

"So, he walks?"

"Not quite. We've got him on attempted murder of a federal agent, multiplied by four, and there's no question that he killed a couple guys inside the house. It's not enough to put him in the chair, but he'll do heavy time. A narc at Raiford, I don't like his odds."

She smiled, the first time since she'd let him in and shown him to the couch. "Too bad."

The Keegan home on Poinciana was predictably immaculate, as if the widow's energy, anger and frustration had been redirected into caring for her son and cleaning house compulsively. Jack did not doubt it for a moment, and he hoped that the conclusion of the case would set her free, at least in part.

The memories would always linger, good and bad together, as they should. In time, with any luck at all, the bad might start to fade and lose its sting. Time had a way of touching up old pictures in the scrapbook of the human mind.

"I guess you had a rough time in the islands."

Fowler thought of Prudence Sullivan and Weldon Glass, one dead, one starting over in a brand-new country with a brand-new name. The lady's testimony would not be required against Rodriguez now, but the DEA and Treasury were going after several local banks connected with the Nassau operation, and she would be helpful there.

"It had its ups and downs."

"I'm glad you're back."

Outside, her son was playing in the yard—toy soldiers with a friend from down the block. They had a battle going near the porch, complete with tanks and childish sound effects.

"How's Tommy?"

"Healing. So am I."

"You're looking good," he said, and meant it from the bottom of his heart.

"You think so?"

"Absolutely."

"I've been thinking...well, you know...about the last time that we talked."

"Me, too."

"Decisions?"

Fowler smiled and shook his head. "You know me, Molly. I was never any good at making up my mind about important things."

"Too bad. It's later than you think."

"I guess that's right," he answered, reaching for his beer and finding it was empty. "Say, you wouldn't have another one of these by any chance?"

She smiled right back at him and said, "I might at that."

The smile felt good. It warmed him up inside.

"Well, there you are."

The Executioner's battle against South American drug lords rages on in Book II of The Medellín Trilogy.

 **EVIL KINGDOM**

The odds of winning are getting slimmer by the minute as the situation heats up. PHOENIX FORCE is trapped in a surprise invasion, one of ABLE TEAM's members is missing, and THE EXECUTIONER is moving in on Colombia's reigning drug czar.

For this powder keg of action, be sure to get your copy of EVIL KINGDOM!

Available in June at your favorite retail outlet, or order your copy now:

THE MEDELLÍN TRILOGY

BOOK I : Blood Rules (THE EXECUTIONER #149)	$3.50 ☐
BOOK II : Evil Kingdom (352-page MACK BOLAN)	$4.50 ☐
BOOK III: Message to Medellín (THE EXECUTIONER #151)	$3.50 ☐
Total Amount	_____
Plus 75¢ postage ($1.00 in Canada)	_____
Total Payable	_____

Please send a check or money order payable to Gold Eagle Books:

In the U.S.
Gold Eagle Books
3010 Walden Ave.
P.O. Box 1325,
Buffalo, NY 14269-1325

In Canada
Gold Eagle Books
P.O. Box 609,
Fort Erie, Ontario
L2A 5X3

Canadian residents add applicable federal and provincial taxes.

Please Print:

Name: _____

Address: _____

City: _____

State/Prov.: _____

Zip/Postal Code: _____

SB23-1

WELCOME TO THE FUTURE—
A FUTURE THAT WELCOMES NO ONE

SURVIVAL 2000

RENEGADE WAR
James McPhee

David Rand's brutal lessons in survival continue in the second book of Gold Eagle's riveting SURVIVAL 2000 series.

Amid a chilling landscape of fiery skies and frozen ground, Rand searches for his kidnapped family, learning to hunt, steal and kill in order to survive in this nightmarish world of the future.

Don't miss this gripping look at the struggle for survival in a future mercilessly altered by destruction.

GOLD
EAGLE

S20002-1

OKLAHOMA'S FINEST—THE MEANEST, TOUGHEST BUNCH OF ROUGH RIDERS—HIT THE SOUTH OF FRANCE....

OKLAHOMA

COMPANY OF HEROES
William Reed

The action-packed, authentic account of America's National Guard continues in BOOK 2 of SOLDIERS OF WAR.

This time, the focus is on Dog Company—the fiercest unit of the Thunderbirds of Oklahoma. They are bound by blood and driven by the fighting spirit that tamed a wild land—and facing tough odds to save the Allied effort in this exciting World War II action.